The Story of a Bad Boy

HARDSCRABBLE BOOKS
Fiction of New England

For a complete list of titles in this series, please see
www.upne.com

THOMAS BAILEY ALDRICH

The STORY of a BAD BOY

Illustrations by A. B. FROST

Introduction by DAVID WATTERS

UNIVERSITY OF NEW HAMPSHIRE PRESS
Durham, New Hampshire
Published by University Press of New England
Hanover and London

UNIVERSITY OF NEW HAMPSHIRE PRESS
Published by University Press of New England,
One Court Street, Lebanon, NH 03766
www.upne.com

Introduction © 1990 by David Watters

Printed in the United States of America   5   4   3

ISBN–13: 978–0–87451–794–1
ISBN–10: 0–87451–794–X

*Published in association with
Strawbery Banke Museum, Portsmouth, NH*

Library of Congress Cataloging-in-Publication Data
Aldrich, Thomas Bailey, 1836–1907
   The story of a bad boy / Thomas Bailey Aldrich; illustrations by A. B. Frost; introduction by David Watters.
   p.   cm. — (Hardscrabble books)
   Reprint. Originally published: Boston : Houghton Mifflin, 1895.
   Summary: These boyhood adventures of a mischievous lad in nineteenth-century New England are based on the author's own experiences.
   ISBN 0–87451–794–X (alk. paper)
   [1. New England — Fiction.] I. Frost, A. B. (Arthur Burdett), 1851–1928, ill. II. Title. III. Series.
PZ7.A37Sto   1996
[Fic]—dc20   96–1905

INTRODUCTION

 Just a few short years after America lost its childhood innocence and half a million young men on the battlefields of the Civil War, Thomas Bailey Aldrich tried to reconstruct a literary all-American boyhood for a modern nation in *The Story of a Bad Boy* (1869). Aldrich's story faithfully chronicles the Portsmouth, New Hampshire, of Aldrich's youth in his grandfather's household from 1849 to 1852. Born in Portsmouth, Aldrich spent his early years in New York and New Orleans as his father pursued an ultimately disastrous career in banking before his death in 1849. In his novel Aldrich invites young readers to share young Tom Bailey's comic vision of a paternalistic, even benevolent slave society in New Orleans, of New England's religiosity, and of spinsters, the Irish, Native Americans, and sailors. The comic vision joins historical conflicts with the pranks of a bad boy to present the antebellum past as a national childhood whose unpleasant moments are to be outgrown and nostalgically recalled. As surely as Manifest Destiny opened new lands for restless American youth, Tom Bailey, and his literary contemporaries, Tom Sawyer, Oliver Optic, Ragged Dick, and Jo March, contributed to the national healing by providing a common ground of childhood memory which transcended regional and social differences.

Like the authors of *Little Women* and *Tom Sawyer*, Aldrich is inseparable from the characters and places of his masterwork. Unlike Louisa May Alcott and Mark Twain, Aldrich mediates childhood through the genial, nostalgic, and ultimately conservative voice of the adult Tom Bailey. His authorial interruptions of the episodic tale may diminish a modern reader's involvement in the escapades of this bad boy. His self-proclaimed "Boston-plated" sensibility of paternalistic capitalism and a mildly racist ethnocentrism kept him from probing too deeply the meaning of his Portsmouth boyhood. These nineteenth-century values contributed to the development of the new, extroverted child-hero that critic Evelyn Geller identifies in the bad-boy, a hero whose "badness" in youth developed into the strong willed entrepreneurial spirit of the adult businessman.

Although Aldrich left the dark side of childhood for later works, such as Henry James's *Turn of the Screw* and J. D. Salinger's *The Catcher in the Rye,* his book has the identifiable marks of a childhood classic. Critic Richard N. Coe argues that in narratives of childhood since the time of St. Augustine archetypal discoveries of evil, sex, love, theater, and death mark the development of the self. All are here, even if evil only slithers forth in the bilking of an ice cream parlor and the seemingly inexplicable resentment of a marginally middle-class Irish boy for his Yankee superiors. For Tom, pugilistic skills, old Yankee money, and family connections soften these blows. Old Rivermouth (the fictional name for Portsmouth) morality vaguely associates each discovery with badness. If the child is to move from conformity to agency through these experiences, then one must be bad to be somebody. Herein lies the boyish pleasure of reading the book.

In our era which proclaims the disappearance of childhood, it may be difficult to understand how revolutionary *The Story of a Bad Boy* was for readers in 1869. Moving a step beyond the tomboy Jo March in Alcott's *Little Women* (1868), Tom Bailey led the way for the satiric unconventionality of Tom Sawyer and the gritty realism of Huck Finn and his alcoholic, abusive Pap. Tom Bailey shows the growing American impatience with the folk wisdom of "the Oldest Inhabitant" of Rivermouth. The sleepy towns and villages of Portsmouth, Concord, and Hannibal are supplanted by the dynamic societies of Boston, New York, and San Francisco. The pious, idealized prigs, to use William Dean Howells's term, of the American Tract Society or Hawthorne's only true nineteenth-century bestseller, "The Gentle Boy," are challenged by the blood and thunder of the sensational, subversive fictions of the popular press. True, Aldrich simply transfers the realism of the adult fiction of his day to children's literature, and as critics Evelyn Geller and Alice Miller Jordan note, he is indebted to Thomas Hughes's *Tom Brown's School Days* (1858) and Jacob Abbot's *Rollo in Scotland* (1858). But one only has to compare the little library Tom Bailey discovers in the Nutter house of the 1840s to that available to young readers in the 1880s to see the decisive turn taken by Aldrich's work.

Tom Bailey consumes the steady sellers of the New England past, from *The Arabian Nights, Robinson Crusoe,* and *Charlotte Temple* to Baxter's *Saints Rest,* the required Sabbath reading that found its way into many a New England garret, but these will not satisfy a "bad" reader for long. In the attic novel-trove, Tom enters an "enchanted realm, where there were no lessons to get and no boys to smash my kite," and he descends "to mystify the staid and slow-going Rivermouthians. . . ." The thrill of reading is matched by the acceleration of pranks Tom's gang plays on the adult world, from schoolyard fights to a fatal boat trip, from a snowball war to the massive explosion of a battery of relic cannon from the War of 1812, from the mock tragedy of an errant arrow in the carriage house production of William Tell, to the real tragedy of the financial collapse and death of Tom's father. Thus the boyhood imagination overturns the antebellum stabilities of Rivermouth society, retrospectively anticipating the cataclysm of the Civil War.

Aldrich imaginatively hopes to resist that change from innocence to experience in a turn worthy of J. M. Barrie's *Peter Pan* when he introduces himself as a bad, but not so bad, boy: "I ought to know, for I am, or rather I was, that boy myself." As critic Virginia L. Wolf points out, this telling ambiguity in the narrator's identification with boyhood sets the mood of the volume. Aldrich concludes that the act of writing has returned him to boyhood, only to make him grow old all over again, "feeling as if I were once more going away from my boyhood."

Aldrich's genial literary genius deserves close inspection. His *Story of a Bad Boy* may suffer by comparison with *The Adventures of Huckleberry Finn,* but one cannot deny the sophistication of his narrative voice. As we are told at the beginning and end of the book, Tom Bailey really isn't such a bad boy at all, but it is not the same Tom Bailey, or for that matter, the same child or adult reader, who ends the book. The act of memory makes Tom Bailey acutely aware of the loss of bad-boy social and narrative freedom as first his grandfather and soon he himself will don the mask of "the Oldest Inhabitant." What boy can avoid encountering a world of loss here? Consider poor Binny Wallace, drowned while fetching lemons from a rowboat, Tom Bailey the "Blighted Being" in melancholic longing for the love of an older cousin, and the death of Tom's father, resonant of the death of that national father, Lincoln. All contribute to the recognition of the conflagratory ephemerality of America for the reader who knows that the patriotic reminiscences of Grandfather Nutter's exploits in 1812 and the fireworks and guns of the Fourth of July celebrations turned bloodily real in 1861.

Despite the presence of a benevolent grandfather and sailor Ben, the father's absence is everywhere; Tom confesses "a want which I have experienced at every step in life from boyhood to manhood." The narrator creates a place seemingly out of time in order to bring the child reader to an intense awareness of the passage of time. Tom may have learned this fictional technique from the mirror of aged storyteller Dame Jocelyn: "When it reflected your face, you had the singular pleasure of not recognizing yourself."

Perhaps all that is left, then, is that old Nutter home, the old village or town, or for those boys who have neither, this house of fiction to which one can return in repose to be very safely bad. Admittedly, this was and is a boy's book, populated with stereotypical females—the domestic Irish servant Kitty Collins, the spinster Aunt Abigail, the Widow Conway. As such it should be significant for feminist critics of the anxious masculinity of post-Civil War America. The young

Tom Bailey's crush on his pretty nineteen-year-old cousin is rendered in comically painful conversation and description, but the old Tom Bailey suggests his ensuing melancholia persists in defining his adult sexuality. He projects his "bad-boy" sexuality onto her eldest son, imagined to be a fourteen-year-old "young villain." The male world of sailor Ben's seaside cabin seems safer, for this marginal figure can mediate between boyhood and adulthood.

Aldrich captures the troubling autobiographical representation of the childhood self in a wonderful image; young Tom is "a little fellow who, when I strive to recall him, appears to me like a reduced ghost of my present self." Absent the verbal and symbolic pyrotechnics of Twain, and the deceptively subtle psychology of Alcott, Aldrich's style rises and falls like the tides of Portsmouth, at one time a placid dreamscape with scarcely a ripple on the surface, at another revealing the barnacled broken-down wharves of the Old New England psyche which still make for a dangerous passage for those venturing from Rivermouth to the open sea.

Portsmouth also plays a leading role in *The Story of a Bad Boy*. Aldrich's shares with the local color writers what anthropologist Clifford Geertz calls local knowledge which interweaves community, place, and history. His descriptions of the world of Portsmouth deserve the attention given to the seacoast classics by Harriet Beecher Stowe, Sarah Orne Jewett, and Celia Thaxter. Aldrich notes ironically, "The harbor is so fine that the largest ships can sail directly up to the wharves and drop anchor. Only they do not." Nevertheless, it is the old town which has a haunting resonance in its local knowledge. "It is strange how memory clings to some things," and without those uniquely Portsmouth things, can Tom Bailey or Tom Aldrich truly exist? One can take this book in hand and rediscover the Portsmouth of the 1840s and most especially, the Aldrich House itself. By luck and prescient efforts in historic preservation, the house exists much as Aldrich knew it at his death in 1907. "Imagine a low-studded structure, with a wide hall running through the middle," and then discover the house there just as imagined. His local color writing is at its finest in the word portraits of the house, school, sailor Ben's cabin, and the river itself. This gallery of a Victorian life preserves for the appreciative reader the childhood of not such a bad boy.

Aldrich's *The Story of a Bad Boy* (1869) reached 75,000 subscribers when published in Lucy Larcom's *Our Young Folks: An Illustrated Magazine for Boys and Girls,* and then it appeared in 47 editions by the time of Aldrich's collected works in 1897. Despite its immense circulation, it is now chiefly known to literary historians as a minor children's classic, and Aldrich's reputation as a poet, novelist, essayist, and editor of the *Atlantic Monthly,* who once ranked with his friends Twain and William Dean Howells, has suffered neglect. It is time to rediscover this work for its invention of the "bad-boy" genre and for its witty and charming contribution to local color literature. *The Story of a Bad Boy* offers to contemporary readers a place in time which reaffirms the human value of one boy's life.

Durham, N.H.   *David Watters*
March 1990

An Aldrich Chronology

1836   Born in Portsmouth, NH, on November 11.

1841–46   The Aldrich family in New York.

1846–49   Residence in New Orleans; father dies in Memphis.

1849–52   TBA returns to Portsmouth home of grandfather to prepare for entrance to Harvard.

1852–55   TBA employed by uncle Charles Frost in NYC; writes poetry.

1855–64   Publishes *The Bells: A Collection of Chimes;* works as critic and editor for magazines.

1865   Marries Miss Lillian Woodman; friend of Edwin Booth and literary figures in NYC; publishes *The Poems of Thomas Bailey Aldrich.*

1866   Moves to Boston to edit *Every Saturday.*

1868   Twins Charles and Talbot born one day after completion of *The Story of a Bad Boy.*

1869   *The Story of a Bad Boy* published.

1873–1903   Publishes novels, travel sketches; edits *The Young Folks' Literary Selections from the Choicest Literature of All Lands,* 20 vols.

1881–90   Reaches peak of fame as editor of *The Atlantic Monthly.*

1897   *The Writings of Thomas Bailey Aldrich,* 8 vols.

1904   Charles Aldrich dies of tuberculosis.

1907   TBA dies, March 19.

1907   Aldrich house on Court Street purchased and restored by the Thomas Bailey Aldrich Memorial Association.

1908   Dedication of the Aldrich Memorial on June 30.

1979   Aldrich house and garden given by the Memorial Association to Strawbery Banke Museum.

1988   Aldrich museum given by the Memorial Association to Strawbery Banke Museum.

A Note on the Illustrations

A. B. Frost's classic illustrations are a perfect accompaniment to Aldrich's style. Frost (1851–1928) was the most popular illustrator of his day, whose work was featured in *Harper's,* his own collections, Lewis Carroll's *Rhyme? and Reason?* (1883), and five of Joel Chandler Harris's Uncle Remus collections.

A Note on this Edition

Thomas Bailey Aldrich's boyhood home on Court Street in Portsmouth, described in *The Story of a Bad Boy* as the "Nutter House," was restored and furnished in 1907–08 to evoke the descriptions given in the novel. At the same time, the Aldrich Memorial Association erected a fireproof brick museum to house Aldrich's books, manuscripts, and memorabilia, and planted the garden in back of the house with flowers mentioned in Aldrich's poems. One of the first historic house restorations in America, the Aldrich Memorial has remained essentially unchanged. Today, it is part of Strawbery Banke and is open to the public from May 1 through October 31. Our goal in presenting *The Story of a Bad Boy* to a new generation of readers and museum visitors is to share the pleasures of this novel and the memorial it spawned and to underscore the importance of both in American literature and historic preservation.

Gerald W. R. Ward
Curator, Strawbery Banke Museum

" My name's Tom Bailey ; what's your name ? "

THE STORY OF
A BAD BOY

BY THOMAS BAILEY ALDRICH

ILLUSTRATED BY

A. B. FROST

BOSTON AND NEW YORK

HOUGHTON, MIFFLIN AND COMPANY

The Riverside Press, Cambridge

M DCCC XCV

The Riverside Press, Cambridge, Mass., U. S. A.
Electrotyped and Printed by H. O. Houghton & Co.

A PREFACE, IN WHICH THE AUTHOR DECLINES TO WRITE ONE

 THE Publishers of the present new edition of THE STORY OF A BAD BOY have requested my agency in the matter of procuring from the author a few lines by way of introduction. It seems to me that the Bad Boy requires no introduction to a public that has tolerated him for upwards of twenty years. Moreover, I am no believer in prefaces. The author who has not been able in the course of several hundred pages to say what he had to say is not likely to accomplish that feat in narrower compass. On consulting with the Bad Boy, I find this to be the view which he himself entertains. He claims that he faithfully performed the modest task he undertook, and is not con-

PREFACE

scious that anything in the narrative requires elucidation. As he concerned himself with little that did not come within the sphere of his own experience, he ran less risk of making mistakes than if he had attempted to write pure fiction. A generous destiny provided him with ample materials for his autobiography, and he invented next to nothing. The statement of this fact incidentally and economically answers the fifteen hundred or two thousand insidious letters which have been addressed to him by autograph-hunters desiring to know whether " The Story of a Bad Boy " was a true story.

These are points, however, on which the author would probably not touch, could he be induced to write a preface. He would deal, rather, with the subsequent fate of the characters who lend what life there is to his little seaport comedy. With one exception they all have made their exit from that larger stage on which they moved more or less successfully. The exception is the Hon. Pepper

Whitcomb. The newspapers, which relieve
our Chief Magistrates from the embarrass-
ment of selecting cabinet officers, foreign
ministers, collectors of the port, and other
high public functionaries — the newspapers,
I repeat, are at the present moment engaged
in putting Pepper Whitcomb into the next
vacancy that may occur on the bench of the
Supreme Court of the United States. The
historian of Rivermouth could have made
much of this dignified circumstance, and
much, also, of the singular fact that the old
Temple Grammar School building was destroyed by fire, a number of years ago, in
precisely the manner foretold in the story :
a coincidence worth dwelling on. Perhaps,
too, the author, with the chronic weakness
peculiar to preface-writers — that sudden
impulse which seizes them to give their own
case away — might have been led to confess
a doubt touching his wisdom in calling the
book " The Story of a *Bad* Boy." He wished
simply to draw a line at the start between

his hero — a natural, actual boy — and that unwholesome and altogether improbable little prig which had hitherto been held up as an example to the young. The title of the volume has doubtless turned aside many excellent persons who would have found nothing seriously reprehensible in the volume itself. On the other hand, this lurid title may have invited the curiosity of the vicious and depraved, and trapped them into reading an entirely harmless story. In which case the author may felicitate himself on sowing a seed in the wider field, for the vicious outnumber the virtuous ten to one. Besides, the virtuous need no missionary.

As the author has never evinced the faintest regret in connection with the title chosen, he probably feels none, and it would be idle on my part to give further chase to a mere conjecture.

The poet Wordsworth, assisted by Plautus, maintains — to the everlasting confusion of Mr. Darwin — that "the good die first."

Perhaps this explains why the Bad Boy has survived so many good boys in the juvenile literature of the last two decades. It only partly explains it, however. The secret of his persistence may be stated without casting any shadow upon the general respectability of his character. Indeed, the secret was long ago kindly disclosed by Mr. Howells [1] when he said: " No one else seems to have thought of telling the story of a boy's life with so great desire to show what a boy's life is, and with so little purpose of teaching what it should be; certainly no one else has thought of doing this for the American boy."

At the period when the author penned these chapters he was far enough away from his boyhood to regard it in retrospect, and yet not so far removed as to be beyond the lightest touch of its glamour. His attitude was wholly without self-consciousness; no photographer of manners had told him to " look natural; " he did not have one eye on

[1] In *The Atlantic Monthly* for January, 1870.

his inkstand and the other on his public.
He had a message, such as it was, and he
delivered it with as good grace as he could.
If he wrote with little art, he wrote with sufficient sincerity, and it so chanced that he
appealed directly not only to the sense of
youthful readers, but to the sympathy of such
men and women as still remembered that
they once were young.

To these two classes the author again offers his unpretentious chronicle, now enriched
by sixty designs from the pencil of Mr. A. B.
Frost, but otherwise unchanged. The writer
tells me that in supervising the sheets for
the press he has a hundred times been
tempted to recast a page or a paragraph;
but there was a morning bloom upon the
faulty text, a bloom that he could not touch
without destroying — a nameless quality of
unknowing youth, impossible to recapture,
and for the lack of which no later art could
compensate.   T. B. A.

The Crags,
Tenant's Harbor, Maine,
1894.

CONTENTS

LIST OF ILLUSTRATIONS

THE STORY OF A BAD BOY

CHAPTER I

IN WHICH I INTRODUCE MYSELF

Not a Cherub

THIS is the story of a bad boy. Well, not such a very bad, but a pretty bad boy; and I ought to know, for I am, or rather I was, that boy myself.

Lest the title should mislead the reader, I hasten to assure him here that I have no dark confessions to make. I call my story the story of a bad boy, partly to distinguish myself from those faultless young gentlemen who generally figure in narratives of this kind, and partly because I really was *not* a cherub. I may truthfully say I was an amiable, impulsive lad, blessed with fine digestive powers, and no hypocrite. I did not want to be an angel and with the angels stand; I did not think the missionary tracts presented to me by the Rev. Wibird Hawkins were half so nice as Robinson Crusoe ; and I failed to send my little pocket-money to the natives of the Feejee Islands, but spent it royally in peppermint-drops and taffy candy. In short, I was a real human boy, such as you may meet anywhere in New England, and no more like the impossible boy in a story-book than a sound orange is like one that has been sucked dry. But let us begin at the beginning.

Whenever a new scholar came to our school, I used to confront him at recess with the following words : " My name 's Tom Bailey ; what 's your name ? " If the name struck me favorably, I shook hands with the new pupil cordially ; but if it did not, I would turn on my heel, for I was particular on this point. Such names as Higgins, Wiggins, and Spriggins were deadly affronts to my ear ; while Langdon, Wallace, Blake, and the like, were passwords to my confidence and esteem.

Ah me ! some of those dear fellows are rather elderly boys by this time — lawyers, merchants, sea-captains, soldiers, authors, what not ? Phil Adams (a special good name that Adams) is consul at Shanghai, where I picture him to myself with his head closely shaved — he never had too much hair — and a long pigtail hanging down behind. He is married, I hear ; and I hope he and she that was Miss Wang Wang are very happy together, sitting cross-legged over their diminutive cups of

tea in a sky-blue tower hung with bells.   It is so
I think of him ; to me he is henceforth a jeweled
mandarin, talking nothing
but broken China.   Whit-
comb is a judge, sedate and
wise, with spectacles balanced on the bridge of that
remarkable nose which, in
former days, was so plenti-
fully sprinkled with freckles
that the boys christened him
Pepper Whitcomb.   Just to
think of little Pepper Whitcomb being a judge ! What
would he do to me now, I

Judge Pepper Whitcomb

wonder, if I were to sing out " Pepper ! " some
day in court ?   Fred Langdon is in California, in
the native-wine business — he used to make the
best licorice-water *I* ever tasted !   Binny Wallace
sleeps in the Old South Burying-Ground ; and
Jack Harris, too, is dead — Harris, who commanded us boys, of old, in the famous snow-ball
battles of Slatter's Hill.   Was it yesterday I saw
him at the head of his regiment on its way to join
the shattered Army of the Potomac ?   Not yesterday, but six years ago.   It was at the battle
of the Seven Pines.   Gallant Jack Harris, that
never drew rein until he had dashed into the
Rebel battery !   So they found him — lying across
the enemy's guns.

How we have parted, and wandered, and married, and died! I wonder what has become of all the boys who went to the Temple Grammar School at Rivermouth when I was a youngster?

"All, all are gone, the old familiar faces!"

It is with no ungentle hand I summon them back, for a moment, from that Past which has closed upon them and upon me. How pleasantly they live again in my memory! Happy, magical Past, in whose fairy atmosphere even Conway, mine ancient foe, stands forth transfigured, with a sort of dreamy glory encircling his bright red hair!

With the old school formula I begin these sketches of my boyhood. My name is Tom Bailey; what is yours, gentle reader? I take for granted that it is neither Wiggins nor Spriggins, and that we shall get on famously together, and be capital friends forever.

CHAPTER II

IN WHICH I ENTERTAIN PECULIAR VIEWS

I WAS born at Rivermouth, but, before I had a chance to become very well acquainted with that pretty New England town, my parents removed to New Orleans, where my father invested his money so securely in the banking business that he was never able to get more than half of it out again. But of this hereafter.

I was only eighteen months old at the time of the removal, and it did not make much difference to me where I was, because I was so small; but several years later, when my father proposed to take me North to be educated, I had my own peculiar views on the subject.

Black Sam

I instantly kicked over the little negro boy who happened to be standing by me at the moment, and, stamping my foot violently on the floor of the piazza, declared that I would not be taken away to live among a lot of Yankees!

You see I was what is called "a Northern man with Southern principles." I had no recollection of New England : my earliest memories were connected with the South, with Aunt Chloe, my old negro nurse, and with the great ill-kept garden in the centre of which stood our house — a whitewashed brick house it was, with wide verandas — shut out from the street by lines of orange, fig, and magnolia trees. I knew I was born at the North, but hoped nobody would find it out. I looked upon the misfortune as something so shrouded by time and distance that maybe nobody remembered it. I never told my schoolmates I was a Yankee, because they talked about the Yankees in such a scornful way as to make me feel that it was quite a disgrace not to be born in Louisiana, or at least in one of the Border States. And this impression was strengthened by Aunt Chloe, who said, " Dar ain't no gentl'men in the Norf noway," and on one occasion terrified me beyond measure by declaring : "If any of dem mean whites tries to git me away from marster, I's jes' gwine to knock 'em on de head wid a gourd !"

The way this poor creature's eyes flashed, and the tragic air with which she struck at an imaginary " mean white," are among the most vivid things in my memory of those days.

To be frank, my idea of the North was about as accurate as that entertained by the well-educated Englishmen of the present day concerning America. I supposed the inhabitants were divided into two classes — Indians and white people ; that the Indians occasionally dashed down on New York, and scalped any woman or child (giving the preference to children) whom they caught lingering in the outskirts after nightfall; that the white men were either hunters or schoolmasters, and that it was winter pretty much all the year round. The prevailing style of architecture I took to be log-cabins.

With this delightful picture of Northern civilization in my eye, the reader will easily understand my terror at the bare thought of being transported to Rivermouth to school, and possibly will forgive me for kicking over little black Sam, and otherwise misconducting myself, when my father announced his determination to me. As for kicking little Sam — I *always* did that, more or less gently, when anything went wrong with me.

My father was greatly perplexed and troubled by this unusually violent outbreak, and especially by the real consternation which he saw written in every line of my countenance. As little black Sam picked himself up, my father took my hand in his and led me thoughtfully to the library.

I can see him now as he leaned back in the bamboo chair and questioned me. He appeared strangely agitated on learning the nature of my objections to going North, and proceeded at once to knock down all my pine-log houses, and scatter all the Indian tribes with which I had populated the greater portion of the East- ern and Middle States.

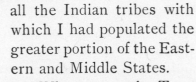

"Who on earth, Tom, has filled your brain with such silly stories?" asked my father, wiping the tears from his eyes.

"Aunt Chloe, sir ; she told me."

"And you really thought your grandfather wore a blanket embroidered with beads, and ornamented his leggings with the scalps of his enemies?"

My Indian Ancestor

"Well, sir, I did n't think that exactly."

"Did n't think that exactly? Tom, you will be the death of me."

He hid his face in his handkerchief, and, when he looked up, he seemed to have been suffering acutely. I was deeply moved myself, though I did not clearly understand what I had said or done to cause him to feel so badly. Perhaps I had hurt his feelings by thinking it even possible that Grand- father Nutter was an Indian warrior.

My father devoted that evening and several subsequent evenings to giving me a clear and succinct
account of New England ; its early struggles, its
progress, and its present condition — faint and confused glimmerings of all which I had obtained at
school, where history had never been a favorite
pursuit of mine.

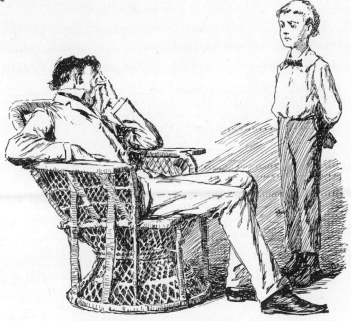

" Tom, you will be the death of me "

I was no longer unwilling to go North ; on the
contrary, the proposed journey to a new world full
of wonders kept me awake nights. I promised
myself all sorts of fun and adventures, though I
was not entirely at rest in my mind touching the

savages, and secretly resolved to go on board the ship — the journey was to be made by sea — with a certain little brass pistol in my trousers pocket, in case of any difficulty with the tribes when we landed at Boston.

I could not get the Indian out of my head. Only a short time previously the Cherokees — or was it the Camanches ? — had been removed from their hunting-grounds in Arkansas ; and in the wilds of the Southwest the red men were still a source of terror to the border settlers. "Trouble with the Indians" was the staple news from Florida published in the New Orleans papers. We were constantly hearing of travelers being attacked and murdered in the interior of that State. If these things were done in Florida, why not in Massachusetts ?

Yet long before the sailing day arrived I was eager to be off. My impatience was increased by the fact that my father had purchased for me a fine little mustang pony, and shipped it to Rivermouth a fortnight previous to the date set for our own departure — for both my parents were to accompany me. The pony (which nearly kicked me out of bed one night in a dream), and my father's promise that he and my mother would come to Rivermouth every other summer, completely resigned me to the situation. The pony's name was *Gitana*, which is the Spanish for gypsy; so I always called her — she was a lady pony — Gypsy.

At last the time came to leave the vine-covered mansion among the orange-trees, to say good-by to little black Sam (I am convinced he was heartily glad to get rid of me), and to part with simple Aunt Chloe, who, in the confusion of her grief, kissed an eyelash into my eye, and then buried her face in the bright bandana turban which she had mounted that morning in honor of our departure.

I fancy them standing by the open garden gate ; the tears are rolling down Aunt Chloe's cheeks ; Sam's six front teeth are glistening like pearls ; I wave my hand to him manfully, then I call out "good-by" in a muffled voice to Aunt Chloe; they and the old home fade away. I am never to see them again!

CHAPTER III

I DO not remember much about the voyage to Boston, for after the first few hours at sea I was dreadfully unwell.

The name of our ship was the "A No. 1, fast-sailing packet Typhoon." I learned afterwards that she sailed fast only in the newspaper advertisements. My father owned one quarter of the Typhoon, and that is why we happened to go in her. I tried to guess which quarter of the ship he owned, and finally concluded it must be the hind quarter — the cabin, in which we had the cosiest of staterooms, with one round window in the roof, and two shelves or boxes nailed up against the wall to sleep in.

There was a good deal of confusion on deck while we were getting under way. The captain shouted orders (to which nobody seemed to pay any attention) through a battered tin trumpet, and grew so red in the face that he reminded me of a scooped-out pumpkin with a lighted candle inside. He swore right and left at the sailors without the slightest regard for their feelings. They did n't mind it a bit, however, but went on singing:

"Heave ho!
With the rum below,
And hurrah for the Spanish Main O!"

I will not be positive about "the Spanish Main,"
but it was hurrah for something O. I considered
them very jolly fel-
lows, and so, indeed,
they were. One
weather-beaten tar in
particular struck my
fancy — a thick-set,
jovial man, about fifty
years of age, with
twinkling blue eyes
and a fringe of gray
hair circling his head
like a crown. As he
took off his tarpaulin
I observed that the
top of his head was

The Captain

quite smooth and flat, as if somebody had sat down
on him when he was very young.

There was something noticeably hearty in this
man's bronzed face, a heartiness that seemed to
extend to his loosely knotted neckerchief. But
what completely won my good will was a picture
of enviable loveliness painted on his left arm. It
was the head of a woman with the body of a fish.
Her flowing hair was of livid green, and she held
a pink comb in one hand. I never saw anything

so beautiful. I determined to know that man. I think I would have given my brass pistol to have had such a picture painted on my arm.

While I stood admiring this work of art, a fat, wheezy steam-tug, with the word AJAX in staring black letters on the paddle-box, came puffing up alongside the Typhoon. It was ridiculously small and conceited, compared with our stately ship. I speculated as to what it was going to do. In a few minutes we were lashed to the little monster, which gave a snort and a shriek, and began backing us out from the levee (wharf) with the greatest ease.

I once saw an ant running away with a piece of cheese eight or ten times larger than itself. I could not help thinking of it, when I found the chubby, smoky-nosed tug-boat towing the Typhoon out into the Mississippi River.

In the middle of the stream we swung round, the current caught us, and away we flew like a great winged bird. Only it did not seem as if *we* were moving. The shore, with the countless steamboats, the tangled rigging of the ships, and the long lines of warehouses, appeared to be gliding away from us.

It was grand sport to stand on the quarter-deck and watch all this. Before long there was nothing to be seen on either side but stretches of low swampy land, covered with stunted cypress-trees, from which drooped delicate streamers of Spanish moss — a fine place for alligators and congo snakes. Here and there we passed a yellow sand-bar, and here and there a snag lifted its nose out of the water like a shark.

" This is your last chance to see the city, Tom," said my father, as we swept round a bend of the river.

I turned and looked. New Orleans was just a colorless mass of something in the distance, and the dome of the St. Charles Hotel, upon which the sun shimmered for a moment, was no bigger than the top of old Aunt Chloe's thimble.

What do I remember next? the gray sky and the fretful blue waters of the Gulf. The steam-tug had long since let slip her hawsers and gone panting away with a derisive scream, as much as to say, " I 've done my duty, now look out for your-self, old Typhoon ! "

The ship seemed quite proud of being left to take care of itself, and, with its huge white sails bulged out, strutted off like a vain turkey. I had been standing by my father near the wheel-house all this while, observing things with that nicety of perception which belongs only to children ; but now the dew began falling, and we went below to have supper.

The fresh fruit and milk, and the slices of cold chicken looked very nice ; yet somehow I had no appetite. There was a general smell of tar about everything. Then the ship gave sudden lurches that made it a matter of uncertainty whether one was going to put his fork to his mouth or into his eye. The tumblers and wineglasses, stuck in a rack over the table, kept clinking and clinking ; and the cabin lamp, suspended by four gilt chains from the ceiling, swayed to and fro crazily. Now the floor seemed to rise, and now it seemed to sink under one's feet like a feather-bed.

There were not more than a dozen passengers on board, including ourselves ; and all of these, excepting a bald-headed old gentleman — a retired sea-captain — disappeared into their staterooms at an early hour of the evening.

After supper was cleared away, my father and  the elderly gentleman, whose name was Captain Truck, played at checkers ; and I amused myself for a while by watching the trouble they had in keeping the men in the proper places. Just at the most exciting point of the game, the ship would careeen, and down would go the white checkers pell-mell among the black. Then my father laughed, but Captain Truck would grow very angry, and vow that he would have won the game in a move or two more, if the confounded old chicken-

Playing Checkers

coop — that 's what he called the ship — had n't lurched.

"I — I think I will go to bed now, please," I said, laying my hand on my father's knee, and feeling exceedingly queer.

It was high time, for the Typhoon was plunging about in the most alarming fashion. I was speedily tucked away in the upper berth, where I felt a trifle more easy at first. My clothes were placed on a narrow shelf at my feet, and it was a great comfort to me to know that my pistol was so handy, for I made no doubt we should fall in with pirates before many hours. This is the last thing I remember with any distinctness. At midnight, as I was afterwards told, we were struck by a gale which never left us until we came in sight of the Massachusetts coast.

For days and days I had no sensible idea of what was going on around me. That we were being hurled somewhere upside-down, and that I did not like it, was about all I knew. I have, indeed, a vague impression that my father used to climb up to the berth and call me his "Ancient Mariner," bidding me cheer up. But the Ancient Mariner was far from cheering up, if I recollect rightly ; and I do not believe that venerable navigator would have cared much if it had been announced to him, through a speaking-trumpet, that "a low, black, suspicious craft, with raking masts, was rapidly bearing down upon us!"

In fact, one morning, I thought that such was the case, for bang! went the big cannon I had noticed in the bow of the ship when we came on board, and which had suggested to me the idea of pirates. Bang! went the gun again in a few seconds. I made a feeble effort to get at my trousers pocket. But the Typhoon was only saluting Cape Cod — the first land sighted by vessels approaching the coast from a southerly direction.

The vessel had ceased to roll, and my seasickness passed away as rapidly as it came. I was all right now, " only a little shaky in my timbers and a little blue about the gills," as Captain Truck remarked to my mother, who, like myself, had been confined to the stateroom during the passage.

At Cape Cod the wind parted company with us without saying as much as " Excuse me;" so we were nearly two days in making the run which in favorable weather is usually accomplished in seven hours. That's what the pilot said.

I was able to go about the ship now, and I lost no time in cultivating the acquaintance of the sailor with the green-haired lady on his arm. I found him in the forecastle — a sort of cellar in the front part of the vessel. He was an agreeable sailor, as I had expected, and we became the best of friends in five minutes.

He had been all over the world two or three times, and knew no end of stories. According to his own account, he must have been shipwrecked

at least twice a year ever since his birth. He had
served under Decatur when that gallant officer
peppered the Algerines and made them promise not

In the Forecastle

to sell their prisoners of war into slavery; he had
worked a gun at the bombardment of Vera Cruz
in the Mexican War, and he had been on Alexan-
der Selkirk's Island more than once. There were

very few things he had not done in a seafaring
way.

"I suppose, sir," I remarked, "that *your* name
is n't Typhoon?"

"Why, Lord love ye, lad, my name's Benjamin
Watson, of Nantucket. But I'm a true blue Ty-
phooner," he added, which increased my respect
for him; I do not know why, and I did not know
then whether Typhoon was the name of a vegeta-
ble or a profession.

Not wishing to be outdone in frankness, I disclosed to him that *my* name was Tom Bailey, upon
which he said he was very glad to hear it.

When we got more intimate, I discovered that
Sailor Ben, as he wished me to call him, was a
perfect walking picture-book. He had two anchors, a star, and a frigate in full sail on his right
arm; a pair of lovely blue hands clasped on his
breast, and I have no doubt that other parts of his
body were illustrated in the same agreeable manner. I imagine he was fond of drawings, and took
this means of gratifying his artistic taste. It was
certainly very ingenious and convenient. A port-
folio might be displaced, or dropped overboard;
but Sailor Ben had his pictures wherever he went,
just as that eminent person in the poem

"With rings on her fingers and bells on her toes"

was accompanied by music on all occasions.

The two hands on his breast, he informed me,
were a tribute to the memory of a dead mess-

mate from whom he had parted years ago — and surely a more touching tribute was never engraved on a tombstone. This caused me to think of my parting with old Aunt Chloe, and I told him I should take it as a great favor indeed if he would paint a pink hand and a black hand on my chest. He said the colors were pricked into the skin with needles, and that the operation was somewhat painful. I assured him, in an off-hand manner, that I did n't mind pain, and begged him to set to work at once.

The simple-hearted fellow, who was probably not a little vain of his skill, took me into the forecastle, and was on the point of complying with my request, when my father happened to look down the gangway — a circumstance that rather interfered with the decorative art.

I did not have another opportunity of conferring alone with Sailor Ben, for the next morning, bright and early, we came in sight of the cupola of the Boston State House.

CHAPTER IV

RIVERMOUTH

It was a beautiful May morning when the Typhoon hauled up at Long Wharf. Whether the Indians were not early risers, or whether they were away just then on a war-path, I could not determine ; but they did not appear in any great force — in fact, did not appear at all.

In the remarkable geography which I never hurt myself with studying at New Orleans was a picture representing the landing of the Pilgrim Fathers at Plymouth. The Pilgrim Fathers, in rather odd hats and coats, are seen approaching the savages ; the savages, in no coats or hats to speak of, are evidently undecided whether to shake hands with the Pilgrim Fathers or to make one grand rush and scalp the entire party. Now this scene had so stamped itself on my mind that, in spite of all my father had said, I was prepared for some such greeting from the aborigines. Nevertheless, I was not sorry to have my expectations unfulfilled. By the way, speaking of the Pilgrim Fathers, I often used to wonder why there was no mention made of the Pilgrim Mothers.

While our trunks were being hoisted from the

hold of the ship, I mounted on the roof of the cabin, and took a critical view of Boston. As we came up the harbor, I had noticed that the houses were huddled together on an immense hill, at the top of which was a large building, the State House, towering proudly above the rest, like an amiable mother-hen surrounded by her brood of many-colored chickens. A closer inspection did not impress me very favorably. The city was not nearly so imposing as New Orleans, which stretches out for miles and miles, in the shape of a crescent, along the banks of the majestic river.

I soon grew tired of looking at the masses of houses, rising above one another in irregular tiers, and was glad my father did not propose to remain long in Boston. As I leaned over the rail in this mood, a measly-looking little boy with no shoes said that if I would come down on the wharf he would lick me for two cents — not an exorbitant price. But I did not go down. I climbed into the rigging, and stared at him. This, as I was rejoiced to observe, so exasperated him that he stood on his head on a pile of boards, in order to pacify himself.

The first train for Rivermouth left at noon. After a late breakfast on board the Typhoon, our trunks were piled upon a baggage-wagon, and ourselves stowed away in a coach, which must have turned at least one hundred corners before it set us down at the railway station.

In less time than it takes to tell it, we were shooting across the country at a fearful rate — now clattering over a bridge, now screaming through a tunnel ; here we cut a flourishing village in two, like a knife, and here we dived into the shadow of a pine forest. Sometimes we glided along the edge of the ocean, and could see the sails of ships twinkling like bits of silver against the horizon ; sometimes we dashed across rocky pasture-lands where stupid-eyed cattle were loafing. It was fun to scare the lazy-looking cows that lay round in groups under the newly budded trees near the railroad track.

We did not pause at any of the little brown stations on the route (they looked just like overgrown black-walnut clocks), though at every one of them a man popped out as if he were worked by machinery, and waved a red flag, and appeared as though he would like to have us stop. But we were an express train, and made no stoppages, excepting once or twice to give the engine a drink.

It is strange how the memory clings to some things. It is over twenty years since I took that first ride to Rivermouth, and yet, oddly enough, I remember as if it were yesterday that, as we passed slowly through the village of Hampton, we saw two boys fighting behind a red barn. There was also a shaggy yellow dog, who looked as if he had begun to unravel, barking himself all up into a knot with excitement. We had only a hur-

ried glimpse of the battle — long enough, however, to see that the combatants were equally matched and very much in earnest. I am ashamed to say how many times since I have speculated as to which boy got licked. Maybe both the small rascals are dead now (not in consequence of the set-to, let us hope), or maybe they are married, and have pug-
nacious urchins
of their own ;
yet to this day
I sometimes
find myself won-
dering how that
fight turned
out.

We had been
riding perhaps
two hours and
a half, when we
shot by a tall
factory with a

A Glimpse of the Battle

chimney resembling a church-steeple ; then the lo-
comotive gave a scream, the engineer rang his bell, and we plunged into the twilight of a long wooden building, open at both ends. Here we stopped, and the conductor, thrusting his head in at the car door, cried out, " Passengers for Rivermouth ! "

At last we had reached our journey's end. On the platform my father shook hands with a straight, brisk old gentleman, whose face was very serene and rosy. He had on a white hat and a long swallow-tailed coat, the collar of which came clear up above his ears. He did not look unlike a Pilgrim Father. This, of course, was grandfather Nutter, at whose house I was born. My mother kissed him a great many times; and I was glad to see him myself, though I naturally did not feel very intimate with a person whom I had not seen since I was eighteen months old.

While we were getting into the double-seated wagon which grandfather Nutter had provided, I took the opportunity of asking after the health of the pony. The pony had arrived all right ten days before, and was in the stable at home, quite anxious to see me.

As we drove through the quiet old town, I thought Rivermouth the prettiest place in the world; and I think so still. The streets are long and wide, shaded by gigantic American elms, whose drooping branches, interlacing here and there, span the avenue with arches graceful enough to be the handiwork of fairies. Many of the houses have small flower-gardens in front, gay in the season with china-asters, and are substantially built, with massive chimney-stacks and protruding eaves. A beautiful river goes rippling by the town, and, after turning and twisting among a lot of tiny islands, empties itself into the sea.

The harbor is so fine that the largest ships can

sail directly up to the wharves and drop anchor. Only they do not. Years ago it was a famous seaport. Princely fortunes were made in the West India trade; and in 1812, when we were at war with Great Britain, any number of privateers were fitted out at Rivermouth to prey upon the merchant vessels of the enemy. Certain people grew suddenly and mysteriously rich. A great many of "the first families" of to-day do not care to trace their pedigree back to the time when their grandsires owned shares in the Matilda Jane, twenty-four guns.

Few ships come to Rivermouth now. Commerce drifted into other ports. The phantom fleet sailed off one day, and never came back again. The crazy old warehouses are empty; and barnacles and eelgrass cling to the piles of the crumbling wharves, where the sunshine lies lovingly, bringing out the faint spicy odor that haunts the place — the ghost of the old dead West India trade.

During our ride from the station, I was struck, of course, only by the general neatness of the houses and the beauty of the elm-trees lining the streets. I describe Rivermouth now as I came to know it afterwards.

Rivermouth is a very ancient town. In my day there existed a tradition among the boys that it was here Christopher Columbus made his first landing on this continent. I remember having the exact spot pointed out to me by Pepper Whitcomb. One thing is certain, Captain John Smith, who afterwards, according to the legend, married Pocahontas — whereby he got Powhatan for a father-in-law — explored the river in 1614, and was much charmed by the beauty of Rivermouth, which at that time was covered with wild strawberry-vines.

Rivermouth figures prominently in all the colonial histories. Every other house in the place has its tradition more or less grim and entertaining. If ghosts could flourish anywhere, there are certain streets in Rivermouth that would be full of them. I do not know of a town with so many old houses. Let us linger, for a moment, in front of the one which the Oldest Inhabitant is always sure to point out to the curious stranger.

It is a square wooden edifice, with gambrel roof and deep-set window-frames. Over the windows and doors there used to be heavy carvings — oak-leaves and acorns, and angels' heads with wings spreading from the ears, oddly jumbled together; but these ornaments and other outward signs of grandeur have long since disappeared. A peculiar interest attaches itself to this house, not because of its age, for it has not been standing quite a century; nor on account of its architecture, which is not striking — but because of the illustrious men who at various periods have occupied its spacious chambers.

In 1770 it was an aristocratic hotel. At the left side of the entrance stood a high post, from which swung the sign of the Earl of Halifax. The landlord was a stanch loyalist — that is to say, he believed in the king, and when the overtaxed colonies determined to throw off the British yoke, the adherents to the Crown held private meetings in one of the back rooms of the tavern. This irritated the rebels, as they were called; and one night they made an attack on the Earl of Halifax, tore down the signboard, broke in the window-sashes, and gave the landlord hardly time to make himself invisible over a fence in the rear.

The Vanishing Landlord

For several months the shattered tavern remained deserted. At last the exiled innkeeper, on promising to do better, was allowed to return; a new sign, bearing the name of William Pitt, the friend of America, swung proudly from the doorpost, and the patriots were appeased. Here it was that the mail-coach from Boston twice a week, for many a year, set down its load of travelers and gossip. For some of the details in this sketch, I am indebted to a recently published chronicle of those times.

It is 1782. The French fleet is lying in the harbor of Rivermouth, and eight of the principal officers, in white uniforms trimmed with gold lace, have taken up their quarters at the sign of the William Pitt. Who is this young and handsome officer now entering the door of the tavern? It is no less a personage than the Marquis Lafayette, who has come all the way from Providence to visit the French gentlemen boarding there. What a gallant-looking cavalier he is, with his quick eyes and coal-black hair! Forty years later he visited the spot again; his locks were gray and his step was feeble, but his heart held its young love for Liberty.

Who is this finely dressed traveler alighting from his coach-and-four, attended by servants in livery? Do you know that sounding name, written in big valorous letters on the Declaration of Independence — written as if by the hand of a giant? Can you not see it now? — JOHN HANCOCK. This is he.

Three young men, with their *valet*, are standing on the door-step of the William Pitt, bowing politely, and inquiring in the most courteous terms in the world if they can be accommodated. It is the time of the French Revolution, and these are three sons of the Duke of Orleans — Louis

Philippe and his two brothers. Louis Philippe never forgot his visit to Rivermouth. Years afterwards, when he was seated on the throne of France, he asked an American lady, who chanced to be at his court, if the pleasant old mansion was still standing.

But a greater and a better man than the king of the French has honored this roof. Here, in 1789, came George Washington, the President of the United States, to pay his final complimentary visit to the State dignitaries. The wainscoted chamber where he slept, and the dining-hall where he entertained his guests, have a certain dignity and sanctity which even the present Irish tenants cannot wholly destroy.

During the period of *my* reign at Rivermouth, an ancient lady, Dame Jocelyn by name, lived in one of the upper rooms of this notable building. She was a dashing young belle at the time of Washington's first visit to the town, and must have been exceedingly coquettish and pretty, judging from a certain portrait on ivory still in the possession of the family. According to Dame Jocelyn, George Washington flirted with her just a little bit — in what a stately and highly finished manner can be imagined.

There was a mirror with a deep filigreed frame hanging over the mantel-piece in this room. The glass was cracked and the quicksilver rubbed off or discolored in many places. When it reflected your face, you had the singular pleasure of not recognizing yourself. It gave your features the appearance of having been run through a mince-meat machine. But what rendered the looking-glass a thing of enchantment to me was a faded green feather, tipped with scarlet, which drooped from the top of the tarnished gilt mouldings. This feather Washington took from the plume of his three-cornered hat, and presented with his own hand to the worshipful Mistress Jocelyn the day he left Rivermouth forever. I wish I could describe the mincing genteel air, and the ill-concealed self-complacency, with which the dear old lady related the incident.

Many a Saturday afternoon have I climbed up the rickety staircase to that dingy room, which always had a flavor of snuff about it, to sit on a stiff-backed chair and listen for hours together to Dame Jocelyn's stories of the olden time. How she would prattle! She was bedridden — poor creature! — and had not been out of the chamber for fourteen years. Meanwhile the world had shot ahead of Dame Jocelyn. The changes that had taken place under her very nose were unknown to this faded, crooning old gentlewoman, whom the eighteenth century had neglected to take away with the rest of its odd traps. She had no patience with new-fangled notions. The old ways and the old times were good enough for her. She had never seen a steam-engine, though she had heard "the dratted thing" screech in the distance. In *her* day, when gentlefolk traveled, they went in their own coaches. She did not see how respectable people could bring themselves down to "riding in a car with rag-tag and bobtail and Lord-knows-who." Poor old aristocrat! the landlord charged her no rent for the room, and the neighbors took turns in supplying her with meals. Towards the close of her life — she lived to be ninety-nine — she grew very fretful and capricious about her food. If she did not chance to fancy what was sent her, she had no hesitation in sending it back to the giver with "Miss Jocelyn's respectful compliments."

"Miss Jocelyn's respectful compliments"

But I have been gossiping too long — and yet not too long if I have impressed upon the reader an idea of what a rusty, delightful old town it was to which I had come to spend the next three or four years of my boyhood.

A drive of twenty minutes from the station brought us to the door-step of Grandfather Nutter's house. What kind of house it was, and what sort of people lived in it, shall be told in another chapter.

CHAPTER V

THE Nutter House — all the more prominent dwellings in Rivermouth are named after somebody ; for instance, there is the Walford House, the Venner House, the Trefethen House, etc., though it by no means follows that they are inhabited by the people whose names they bear — the Nutter House, to resume, has been in our family nearly a hundred years, and is an honor to the builder (an ancestor of ours, I believe), supposing durability to be a merit. If our ancestor *was* a carpenter, he knew his trade. I wish I knew mine as well. Such timber and such workmanship do not often come together in houses built nowadays.

Imagine a low-studded structure, with a wide hall running through the middle. At your right hand, as you enter, stands a tall black mahogany clock, looking like an Egyptian mummy set up on end. On each side of the hall are doors (whose knobs, it must be confessed, do not turn very easily), opening into large rooms wainscoted and rich in wood-carvings about the mantel-pieces and cornices. The walls are covered with pictured

paper, representing landscapes and sea-views.   In
the parlor, for example, this enlivening figure is
repeated all over the room : A group of English
peasants, wearing Italian hats, are dancing on a
lawn that abruptly resolves itself into a sea-beach,
upon which stands a flabby fisherman (nationality
unknown), quietly hauling in what appears to be
a small whale, and totally regardless of the dreadful naval combat going on just beyond the end of
his fishing-rod.   On the other side of the ships is
the mainland again, with the same peasants dancing.   Our ancestors were very worthy people, but
their wall-papers were abominable.

There are neither grates nor stoves in these
quaint chambers, but splendid open chimney-
places, with room enough for the corpulent back-
log to turn over comfortably on the polished and-
irons.   A wide staircase leads from the hall to the
second story, which is arranged much like the first.
Over this is the garret.   I need not tell a New England boy what a museum of curiosities is the garret of a well-regulated New England house of fifty
or sixty years' standing.   Here meet together, as
if by some preconcerted arrangement, all the broken-down chairs of the household, all the spavined
tables, all the seedy hats, all the intoxicated-looking
boots, all the split walking-sticks that have retired
from business, " weary with the march of life."
The pots, the pans, the trunks, the bottles — who
may hope to make an inventory of the number-

less odds and ends collected in this bewildering lumber-room ? But what a place it is to sit of an afternoon with the rain pattering on the roof ! what a place in which to read Gulliver's Travels, or the famous adventures of Rinaldo Rinaldini !

My grandfather's house stood a little back from the main street, in the shadow of two handsome elms, whose overgrown boughs would dash themselves against the gables whenever the wind blew hard. In the rear was a pleasant garden, covering perhaps a quarter of an acre, full of plum-trees and gooseberry-bushes. These trees were old settlers, and are all dead now, excepting one, which bears a purple plum as big as an egg. This tree, as I remark, is still standing, and a more beautiful tree to tumble out of never grew anywhere. In the northwestern corner of the garden were the stables and carriage-house, opening upon a narrow lane. You may imagine that I made an early visit to that locality to inspect Gypsy. Indeed, I paid her a visit every half-hour during the first day of my arrival. At the twenty-fourth visit she trod on my foot rather heavily, as a reminder, probably, that I was wearing out my welcome. She was a knowing little pony, that Gypsy, and I shall have much to say of her in the course of these pages.

Gypsy's quarters were all that could be wished, but nothing among my new surroundings gave me more satisfaction than the cosy sleeping apartment that had been prepared for myself. It was the hall room over the front door.

I had never before had a chamber all to myself, and this one, about twice the size of our state-room on board the Typhoon, was a marvel of neatness and comfort. Pretty chintz curtains hung at the window, and a patch quilt of more colors than were in Joseph's coat covered the little truckle-bed. The pattern of the wall-paper left nothing to be desired in that line. On a gray background were small bunches of leaves, unlike any that ever grew in this world; and on every other bunch perched a yellow-bird,

" A fine black eye "

pitted with crimson spots, as if it had just recovered from a severe attack of the small-pox. That no such bird ever existed did not detract from my admiration of each one. There were two hundred and sixty-eight of these birds in all, not counting those split in two where the paper was badly joined. I counted them once when I was laid up with a fine black eye, and falling asleep immediately dreamed that the whole flock suddenly took wing and flew out of the window. From that time I was never able to regard them as merely inanimate objects.

A wash-stand in the corner, a chest of carved mahogany drawers, a looking-glass in a filigreed frame, and a high-backed chair studded with brass nails like a coffin, constituted the furniture.

Over the head of the bed were two oak shelves, holding perhaps a dozen books — among which were Theodore, or The Peruvians ; Robinson Crusoe ; an odd volume of Tristram Shandy ; Baxter's Saints' Rest, and a fine English edition of the Arabian Nights, with six hundred wood-cuts by Harvey.

Shall I ever forget the hour when I first overhauled these books ? I do not allude especially to Baxter's Saints' Rest, which is far from being a lively work for the young, but to the Arabian Nights, and particularly Robinson Crusoe. The thrill that ran into my fingers' ends then has not run out yet. Many a time did I steal up to this nest of a room, and, taking the dog's-eared volume from its shelf, glide off into an enchanted realm, where there were no lessons to get and no boys to smash my kite. In a lidless trunk in the garret I subsequently unearthed another motley collection of novels and romances, embracing the adventures of Baron Trenck, Jack Sheppard, Don Quixote, Gil Blas, and Charlotte Temple — all of which I fed upon like a bookworm.

I never come across a copy of any of those works without feeling a certain tenderness for the yellow-haired little rascal who used to lean above the magic pages hour after hour, religiously believing every word he read, and no more doubting the reality of Sindbad the Sailor, or the Knight of the Sorrowful Countenance, than he did the existence of his own grandfather.

A Rainy Afternoon in the Garret

Against the wall at the foot of the bed hung a single-barrel shot-gun — placed there by Grandfather Nutter, who knew what a boy loved, if ever a grandfather did. As the trigger of the gun had been accidentally twisted off, it was not, perhaps, the most dangerous weapon that could be placed in the hands of youth. In this maimed condition its bump of destructiveness was much less than that of my small brass pocket-pistol, which I at once proceeded to suspend from one of the nails supporting the fowling-piece, for my vagaries concerning the red man had been entirely dispelled.

Having introduced the reader to the Nutter House, a presentation to the Nutter family naturally follows. The family consisted of my grandfather ; his sister, Miss Abigail Nutter ; and Kitty Collins, the maid-of-all-work.

Grandfather Nutter was a hale, cheery old gentleman, as straight and as bald as an arrow. He had been a sailor in early life ; that is to say, at the age of ten years he fled from the multiplication-table, and ran away to sea. A single voyage satisfied him. There never was but one of our family who did not run away to sea, and this one died at his birth. My grandfather had also been a soldier — a captain of militia in 1812. If I owe the British nation anything, I owe thanks to that particular British soldier who put a musket-ball into the fleshy part of Captain Nutter's leg, causing that noble warrior a slight permanent limp, but offsetting the injury by furnishing him with material for a story which the old gentleman was never weary of telling and I never weary of listening to. The story, in brief, was as follows.

At the breaking out of the war, an English frigate lay for several days off the coast near Rivermouth. A strong fort defended the harbor, and a regiment of minute-men, scattered at various points alongshore, stood ready to repel the boats, should the enemy try to effect a landing. Captain Nutter had charge of a slight earthwork just outside the mouth of the river. Late one thick night the sound of oars was heard ; the sentinel tried to fire off his gun at half-cock, and could not, when Captain Nutter sprung upon the parapet in the pitch darkness, and shouted, " Boat ahoy ! " A musket-shot immediately embedded itself in the calf of his leg. The Captain tumbled into the fort, and the boat, which had probably come in search of water, pulled back to the frigate.

This was my grandfather's only exploit during the war. That his prompt and bold conduct was instrumental in teaching the enemy the hopelessness of attempting to conquer such a people was among the firm beliefs of my boyhood.

At the time I came to Rivermouth my grandfather had retired from active pursuits, and was living at ease on his money, invested principally in shipping. He had been a widower many years ; a maiden sister, the aforesaid Miss Abigail, man-

aging his household. Miss Abigail also managed
her brother, and her brother's servant, and the visitor at her brother's gate — not in a tyrannical

Miss Abigail and Kitty Collins

spirit, but from a philanthropic desire to be useful
to everybody. In person she was tall and angu-
lar ; she had a gray complexion, gray eyes, gray
eyebrows, and generally wore a gray dress. Her
strongest weak point was a belief in the efficacy
of " hot-drops " as a cure for all known diseases.

If there were ever two persons who seemed to

dislike each other, Miss Abigail and Kitty Collins were those persons.   If ever two persons really loved each other, Miss Abigail and Kitty Collins were those persons also.   They were always either skirmishing or having a cup of tea lovingly to-gether.

Miss Abigail was very fond of me, and so was Kitty ; and in the course of their disagreements each let me into the private history of the other.

According to Kitty, it was not originally my grandfather's intention to have Miss Abigail at the head of his domestic establishment.   She had swooped down on him (Kitty's own words), with a band-box in one hand and a faded blue cotton umbrella, still in existence, in the other.   Clad in this singular garb — I do not remember that Kitty alluded to any additional peculiarity of dress — Miss Abigail had made her appearance at the door of the Nutter House on the morning of my grandmother's funeral.   The small amount of bag-gage which the lady brought with her would have led the superficial observer to infer that Miss Abi-gail's visit was limited to a few days.   I run ahead of my story in saying she remained seventeen years! How much longer she would have re-mained can never be definitely known now, as she died at the expiration of that period.

Whether or not my grandfather was quite pleased by this unlooked-for addition to his family is a problem.   He was very kind always to Miss

Abigail, and seldom opposed her; though I think she must have tried his patience sometimes, especially when she interfered with Kitty.

Kitty Collins, or Mrs. Catherine, as she perferred to be called, was descended in a direct line from an extensive family of kings who formerly ruled over Ireland. In consequence of various calamities, among which the failure of the potato-crop may be mentioned, Miss Kitty Collins, in company with several hundred of her countrymen and countrywomen — also descended from kings — came over to America in an emigrant ship, in the year eighteen hundred and something

I do not know what freak of fortune caused the royal exile to turn up at Rivermouth; but turn up she did, a few months after arriving in this country, and was hired by my grandmother to do "general housework" for the modest sum of four shillings and sixpence a week.

Kitty had been living about seven years in my grandfather's family when she unburdened her heart of a secret which had been weighing upon it all that time. It may be said of people, as it is said of nations, "Happy are they that have no history." Kitty had a history, and a pathetic one, I think.

On board the emigrant ship that brought her to America, she became acquainted with a sailor, who, being touched by Kitty's forlorn condition, was very good to her. Long before the end of the

voyage, which had been tedious and perilous, she
was heart-broken at the thought of separating
from her kindly protector; but they were not to
part just yet, for the sailor returned Kitty's affection, and the two were married on their arrival at
port. Kitty's husband — she would never mention his name, but kept it locked in her bosom
like some precious relic — had a considerable sum
of money when the crew were paid off ; and the
young couple — for Kitty was young then — lived
very happily in a lodging-house on South Street,
near the docks.   This was in New York.

The days flew by like hours, and the stocking
in which the little bride kept the funds shrunk
and shrunk, until at last there were only three or
four dollars left in the toe of it.   Then Kitty was
troubled ; for she knew her sailor would have to
go to sea again unless he could get employment
on shore.   This he endeavored to do, but not with
much success.   One morning as usual he kissed
her good day, and set out in search of work.

"Kissed me good-by, and called me his little
Irish lass," sobbed Kitty, telling the story —
"kissed me good-by, and, Heaven help me! I
niver set oi on him nor on the likes of him again."

He never came back.   Day after day dragged
on, night after night, and then the weary weeks.
What had become of him ?   Had he been murdered ? had he fallen into the docks ? had he —
deserted her?   No! she could not believe that ; he

was too brave and tender and true. She could not believe that.   He was dead, dead, or he would come back to her.

Meanwhile the landlord of the lodging-house turned Kitty into the streets, now that " her man" was gone, and the payment of the rent doubtful. She got a place as a servant. The family she lived with shortly moved to Boston, and she accompanied them; then they went abroad, but Kitty would not leave America. Somehow she drifted to Rivermouth, and for seven long years never gave speech to her sorrow, until the kindness of strangers, who had become friends to her, unsealed the heroic lips.

Kitty's story, you may be sure, made my grandparents treat her more kindly than ever. In time she grew to be regarded less as a servant than as a friend in the home circle, sharing its joys and sorrows — a faithful nurse, a willing slave, a happy spirit in spite of all. I fancy I hear her singing over her work in the kitchen, pausing from time to time to make some witty reply to Miss Abigail — for Kitty, like all her race, had a vein of unconscious humor. Her bright honest face comes to me out from the past, the light and life of the Nutter House when I was a boy at Rivermouth.

CHAPTER VI

LIGHTS AND SHADOWS

THE first shadow that fell upon me in my new home was caused by the return of my parents to New Orleans. Their visit was cut short by business which required my father's presence in Natchez, where he was establishing a branch of the banking-house. When they had gone, a sense of loneliness such as I had never dreamed of filled my young breast. I crept away to the stable, and, throwing my arms about Gypsy's neck, sobbed aloud. She too had come from the sunny South, and was now a stranger in a strange land.

The little mare seemed to realize our situation, and gave me all the sympathy I could ask, repeatedly rubbing her soft nose over my face and lapping up my salt tears with evident relish.

When night came, I felt still more lonesome. My grandfather sat in his armchair the greater part of the evening, reading the Rivermouth Barnacle, the local newspaper. There was no gas in those days, and the Captain read by the aid of a small block-tin lamp, which he held in one hand. I observed that he had a habit of dropping off into a doze every three or four minutes, and I for-

Waiting for the Conflagration

got my homesickness at intervals in watching
him. Two or three times, to my vast amusement,
he scorched the edges of the newspaper with the
wick of the lamp ; and at about half past eight
o'clock I had the satisfaction — I am sorry to confess it was a satisfaction — of seeing the Rivermouth Barnacle in flames.

My grandfather leisurely extinguished the fire
with his hands, and Miss Abigail, who sat near
a low table, knitting by the light of an astral lamp,
did not even look up. She was quite used to this
catastrophe.

There was little or no conversation during the
evening. In fact, I do not remember that any
one spoke at all, excepting once, when the Captain
remarked, in a meditative manner, that my parents
"must have reached New York by this time ; " at
at which supposition I nearly strangled myself in
attempting to intercept a sob.

The monotonous "click click" of Miss Abigail's needles made me nervous after a while, and
finally drove me out of the sitting-room into the
kitchen, where Kitty caused me to laugh by saying Miss Abigail thought that what I needed was
"a good dose of hot-drops" — a remedy she was
forever ready to administer in all emergencies.
If a boy broke his leg, or lost his mother, I believe
Miss Abigail would have given him hot-drops.

Kitty laid herself out to be entertaining. She
told me several funny Irish stories, and described

some of the odd people living in the town ; but, in the midst of her comicalities, the tears would involuntarily ooze out of my eyes, though I was not a lad much addicted to weeping. Then Kitty would put her arms around me, and tell me not to mind it — that it was not as if I had been left alone in a foreign land with no one to care for me, like a poor girl whom she had once known. I brightened up before long, and told Kitty all about the Typhoon and the old seaman, whose name I tried in vain to recall, and was obliged to fall back on plain Sailor Ben.

I was glad when ten o'clock came, the bedtime for young folks, and old folks too, at the Nutter House. Alone in the hall-chamber I had my cry out, once for all, moistening the pillow to such an extent that I was obliged to turn it over to find a dry spot to go to sleep on.

My grandfather wisely concluded to put me to school at once. If I had been permitted to go mooning about the house and stables, I should have kept my discontent alive for months. The next morning, accordingly, he took me by the hand, and we set forth for the academy, which was located at the farther end of the town.

The Temple School was a two-story brick building, standing in the centre of a great square piece of land, surrounded by a high picket fence. There were three or four sickly trees, but no grass, in this inclosure, which had been worn smooth and hard by the tread of multitudinous feet. I noticed here and there small holes scooped in the ground, indicating that it was the season for marbles. A better playground for base-ball could not have been devised.

On reaching the schoolhouse door, the Captain inquired for Mr. Grim- shaw. The boy who an- swered our knock ush- ered us into a side room, and in a few minutes — during which my eye took in forty-two caps hung on forty-two wooden pegs — Mr. Grimshaw made his appearance. He was a slender man, with white, fragile hands, and eyes that glanced half a dozen different ways at once — a habit probably acquired from watching the boys.

Mr. Grimshaw

After a brief consultation, my grandfather pat- ted me on the head and left me in charge of this gentleman, who seated himself in front of me and proceeded to sound the depth, or more properly speaking, the shallowness, of my attainments. I suspect that my historical information rather star- tled him. I recollect I gave him to understand that Richard III. was the last king of England.

This ordeal over, Mr. Grimshaw rose and bade

me follow him. A door opened, and I stood in the blaze of forty-two pairs of upturned eyes. I was a cool hand for my age, but I lacked the boldness to face this battery without wincing. In a sort of dazed way I stumbled after Mr. Grimshaw down a narrow aisle between two rows of desks, and shyly took the seat pointed out to me.

The faint buzz that had floated over the school-room at our entrance died away, and the interrupted lessons were resumed. By degrees I recovered my coolness, and ventured to look around me.

The owners of the forty-two caps were seated at small green desks like the one assigned to me. The desks were arranged in six rows, with spaces between just wide enough to prevent the boys' whispering. A blackboard set into the wall extended clear across the end of the room ; on a raised platform near the door stood the master's table; and directly in front of this was a recitation bench capable of seating fifteen or twenty pupils. A pair of globes, tattooed with dragons and winged horses, occupied a shelf between two windows, which was so high from the floor that nothing but a giraffe could have looked out of them.

Having possessed myself of these details, I scrutinized my new acquaintances with unconcealed curiosity, instinctively selecting my friends and picking out my enemies — and in only two cases did I mistake my man.

A sallow boy with bright red hair, sitting in the fourth row, shook his fist at me furtively several times during the morning. I had a presentiment I should have trouble with that boy some day — a presentiment subsequently realized.

On my left was a chubby little fellow with a great many freckles (this was Pepper Whitcomb), who made some mysterious motions to me. I did not understand them, but, as they were clearly of a pacific nature, I winked my eye at him. This appeared to be satisfactory, for he then went on with his studies. At recess he gave me the core of his apple, though there were several applicants for it.

Presently a boy in a loose olive-green jacket with two rows of brass buttons, held up a folded paper behind his slate, intimating that it was intended for me. The paper was passed skillfully from desk to desk until it reached my hands. On opening the scrap, I found that it contained a small piece of molasses candy in an extremely humid state. This was certainly kind. I nodded my acknowledgments and hastily slipped the delicacy into my mouth. In a second I felt my tongue grow red-hot with cayenne pepper.

My face must have assumed a comical expression, for the boy in the olive-green jacket gave an hysterical laugh, for which he was instantly punished by Mr. Grimshaw. I swallowed the fiery candy, though it brought the water to my eyes, and managed to look so unconcerned that I was the only pupil in the form who escaped questioning as to the cause of Marden's misdemeanor. Marden was his name.

Swallowing the Candy

Nothing else occurred that morning to interrupt the exercises, excepting that a boy in the reading class threw us all into convulsions by calling Absalom *A-bol'-som,* — "Abol'som, O my son Abol'som!" I laughed as loud as any one, but I am not so sure that I should not have pronounced it Abol'som myself.

At recess several of the scholars came to my desk and shook hands with me, Mr. Grimshaw having previously introduced me to Phil Adams, charging him to see that I got into no trouble. My new acquaintances suggested that we should go to the playground. We were no sooner out of doors than the boy with the red hair thrust his way through the crowd and placed himself at my side.

"I say, youngster, if you 're comin' to this school you 've got to toe the mark."

I did not see any mark to toe, and did not understand what he meant; but I replied politely, that, if it was the custom of the school, I should be happy to toe the mark, if he would point it out to me.

"I don't want any of your sarse," said the boy, scowling.

"Look here, Conway!" cried a clear voice from the other side of the playground, "you let young Bailey alone. He's a stranger here, and might be afraid of you, and thrash you. Why do you always throw yourself in the way of getting thrashed?"

I turned to the speaker, who by this time had reached the spot where we stood. Conway slunk off, favoring me with a parting scowl of defiance. I gave my hand to the boy who had befriended me — his name was Jack Harris — and thanked him for his good-will.

"I tell you what it is, Bailey," he said, returning my pressure good-naturedly, "you'll have to fight Conway before the quarter ends, or you'll have no rest. That fellow is always hankering after a licking, and of course you'll give him one by and by; but what's the use of hurrying up an unpleasant job? Let's have some base-ball. By the way, Bailey, you were a good kid not to let on to Grimshaw about the candy. Charley Marden would have caught it twice as heavy. He's sorry he played the joke on you, and told me to tell you so. Hallo, Blake! where are the bats?"

This was addressed to a handsome, frank-looking lad of about my own age, who was engaged just then in cutting his initials on the bark of a tree near the schoolhouse. Blake shut up his penknife and went off to get the bats.

During the game which ensued I made the acquaintance of Charley Marden, and Binny Wallace, Pepper Whitcomb, Harry Blake, and Fred Langdon. These boys, none of them more than a year or two older than I (Binny Wallace was younger), were ever after my chosen comrades. Phil Adams and Jack Harris were considerably our seniors, and though they always treated us "kids" very kindly, they generally went with another set. Of course, before long I knew all the Temple boys more or less intimately, but the five I have named were my constant companions.

My first day at the Temple Grammar School was on the whole satisfactory. I had made several warm friends, and only two permanent enemies — Conway and his echo, Seth Rodgers ; for these two always went together like a deranged stomach and a headache.

Before the end of the week I had my studies well in hand. I was a little ashamed at finding myself at the foot of the various classes, and secretly determined to deserve promotion. The school was an admirable one. I might make this part of my story more entertaining by picturing Mr. Grimshaw as a tyrant with a red nose and a large stick ; but unfortunately for the purposes of sensational narrative, Mr. Grimshaw was a quiet, kind-hearted gentleman. Though a rigid disciplinarian, he had a keen sense of justice, was a good reader of character, and the boys respected him.

There were two other teachers — a French tutor
and a writing-master, who visited the school twice
a week. On Wednesdays and Saturdays we were
dismissed at noon, and these half-holidays were
the brightest epochs of my existence.

Daily contact with boys who had not been
brought up as gently as I worked an immediate,
and, in some respects, a beneficial change in my
character. I had the nonsense taken out of me, as
the saying is — some of the nonsense, at least.
I became more manly and self-reliant. I discovered
that the world was not created exclusively on my
account. In New Orleans I labored under the delusion that it was. Having neither brother nor
sister to give up to at home, and being, moreover,
the largest pupil at school there, my will had seldom been opposed. At Rivermouth matters were
different, and I was not long in adapting myself to
the altered circumstances. Of course I got many
severe rubs, often unconsciously given ; but I had
the sense to see that I was all the better for them.
My social relations with my new schoolfellows
were the pleasantest possible. There was always
some exciting excursion on foot — a ramble through
the pine woods, a visit to the Devil's Pulpit, a high
cliff in the neighborhood — or a surreptitious row
on the river, involving an exploration of a group of
diminutive islands, upon one of which we pitched
a tent and played we were the Spanish sailors who

got wrecked there years ago. But the endless pine forest that skirted the town was our favorite haunt. There was a great green pond hidden somewhere in its depths, inhabited by a monstrous colony of turtles. Harry Blake, who had an eccentric passion for carving his name on everything, never let a captured turtle slip through his fingers without leaving his mark engraved on its shell. He must have lettered about two thousand from first to last. We used to call them Harry Blake's sheep.

These turtles were of a discontented and migratory turn of mind, and we frequently encountered two or three of them on the cross-roads several miles from their ancestral mud. Unspeakable was our delight whenever we discovered one soberly walking off with Harry Blake's initials! I have no doubt there are, at this moment, fat ancient turtles wandering about that gummy woodland with **H. B.** neatly cut on their venerable backs.

It soon became a custom among my playmates to make our barn their rendezvous. Gypsy proved a strong attraction. Captain Nutter bought me a little two-wheeled cart, which she drew quite nicely, after kicking out the dasher and breaking the shafts once or twice. With our lunch-baskets and fishing-tackle stowed away under the seat, we used to start off early in the afternoon for the seashore, where there were countless marvels in the shape of shells, mosses, and kelp. Gypsy enjoyed the sport as keenly as any of us, even going so far, one day, as to trot down the beach into the sea where we were bathing. As she took the cart with her, our provisions were not much improved. I shall never forget how squash-pie tastes after being soused in the Atlantic Ocean. Soda-crackers dipped in salt water are palatable, but not squash-pie.

There was a good deal of wet weather during those first six weeks at Rivermouth, and we set ourselves at work to find some in-door amusement for our half-holidays. It was all very well for Amadis de Gaul and Don Quixote not to mind the rain ; they had iron overcoats, and were not, from all we can learn, subject to croup and the guidance of their grandfathers. Our case was different.

"Now, boys, what shall we do ? " I asked, addressing a thoughtful conclave of seven, assembled in our barn one dismal rainy afternoon.

"Let's have a theatre," suggested Binny Wallace.

The very thing ! But where ? The loft of the stable was ready to burst with hay provided for Gypsy, but the long room over the carriage-house was unoccupied. The place of all places ! My managerial eye saw at a glance its capabilities for a theatre. I had been to the play a great many times in New Orleans, and was wise in matters pertaining to the drama. So here, in due time, was set up some extraordinary scenery of my own painting. The curtain, I recollect, though it worked smoothly enough on other occasions, invariably hitched during the performances ; and it often required the united energies of the Prince of Denmark, the King, and the Grave-digger, with an occasional hand from " the fair Ophelia " (Pepper Whitcomb in a low - necked dress), to hoist that bit of green cambric.

The theatre, however, was a success, so far as it went. I retired from the business with no fewer than fifteen hundred pins, after deducting the headless, the pointless, and the crooked pins with which our doorkeeper frequently got "stuck." From first to last we took in a great deal of this counterfeit money. The price of admission to the " Rivermouth Theatre" was twenty pins. I played all the principal parts myself — not that I was a finer actor than the other boys, but because I owned the establishment.

At the tenth representation, my dramatic career was brought to a close by an unfortunate circumstance. We were playing the drama of " William Tell the Hero of Switzerland." Of course I was William Tell, in spite of Fred Langdon, who wanted to act that character himself. I would not let him, so he withdrew from the company, taking the only bow and arrow we had. I made a cross-bow out of a piece of whalebone, and did very well without him. We had reached that exciting scene where Gessler, the Austrian tyrant, commands Tell to shoot the apple from his son's head. Pepper Whitcomb, who played all the juvenile and women parts, was my son. To guard against mischance, a piece of pasteboard was fastened by a handkerchief over the upper portion of Whitcomb's face, while the arrow to be used was sewed up in a strip of flannel. I was a capital marksman, and

The Drama of William Tell

the big apple, only two yards distant, turned its russet cheek fairly towards me.

I can see poor little Pepper now, as he stood without flinching, waiting for me to perform my great feat. I raised the cross-bow amid the breathless silence of the crowded audience — consisting of seven boys and three girls, exclusive of Kitty Collins, who insisted on paying her way in with a clothes-pin. I raised the cross-bow, I repeat.

Twang! went the whipcord ; but, alas! instead of hitting the apple, the arrow flew right into Pepper Whitcomb's mouth, which happened to be open at the time, and destroyed my aim.

I shall never be able to banish that awful moment from my memory. Pepper's roar, expressive of astonishment, indignation, and pain, is still ringing in my ears. I looked upon him as a corpse, and, glancing not far into the dreary future, pictured myself led forth to execution in the presence of the very same spectators then assembled.

Luckily poor Pepper was not seriously hurt ; but Grandfather Nutter, appearing in the midst of the confusion (attracted by the howls of young Tell), issued an injunction against all theatricals thereafter, and the place was closed ; not, however, without a farewell speech from me, in which I said that this would have been the proudest moment of my life if I had not hit Pepper Whitcomb in the mouth. Whereupon the audience (assisted, I am glad to state, by Pepper) cried " Hear! hear! " I then attributed the accident to Pepper himself, whose mouth, being open at the instant I fired, acted upon the arrow much after the fashion of a whirlpool, and drew in the fatal shaft. I was about to explain how a comparatively small maelstrom could suck in the largest ship, when the curtain fell of its own accord, amid the shouts of the audience.

This was my last appearance on any stage. It was some time, though, before I heard the end of the William Tell business. Malicious little boys who had not been allowed to buy tickets to my theatre used to cry out after me in the street :

> " ' Who killed Cock Robin ? '
> ' I,' said the sparrer,
> ' With my bow and arrer,
> I killed Cock Robin ! ' "

The sarcasm of this verse was more than I could stand. And it made Pepper Whitcomb pretty mad to be called Cock Robin, I can tell you !

So the days glided on, with fewer clouds and more sunshine than fall to the lot of most boys. Conway was certainly a cloud. Within school-bounds he seldom ventured to be aggressive ; but whenever we met about town he never failed to brush against me, or pull my cap over my eyes, or drive me distracted by inquiring after my family in New Orleans, always alluding to them as highly respectable colored people.

Jack Harris was right when he said Conway would give me no rest until I fought him. I felt it was ordained ages before our birth that we should meet on this planet and fight. With the view of not running counter to destiny, I quietly prepared myself for the impending conflict. The scene of my dramatic triumphs was turned into a gymnasium for this purpose, though I did not openly avow the fact to the boys. By persistently standing on my head, raising heavy weights, and going hand over hand up a ladder, I developed my muscle until my little body was as tough as a hickory knot and as supple as tripe. I also took occasional lessons in the noble art of self-defense, under the tuition of Phil Adams.

I brooded over the matter until the idea of fighting Conway became a part of me. I fought him in imagination during school-hours ; I dreamed of fighting with him at night, when he would suddenly expand into a giant twelve feet high, and then as suddenly shrink into a pygmy so small that I could not hit him. In this latter shape he would get into my hair, or pop into my waistcoat-pocket, treating me with as little ceremony as the Lilliputians showed Captain Lemuel Gulliver — all of which was not pleasant, to be sure. On the whole, Conway was a cloud.

And then I had a cloud at home. It was not Grandfather Nutter, nor Miss Abigail, nor Kitty Collins, though they all helped to compose it. It was a vague, funereal, impalpable something which no amount of gymnastic training would enable me to knock over. It was Sunday. If ever I have a boy to bring up in the way he should go, I intend to make Sunday a cheerful day to him. Sunday was *not* a cheerful day at the Nutter House. You shall judge for yourself.

It is Sunday morning. I should premise by saying that the deep gloom which has settled over everything set in like a heavy fog early on Saturday evening.

At seven o'clock my grandfather comes smile-
lessly down stairs. He is dressed in black, and
looks as if he had lost all his friends during the
night. Miss Abigail, also in black, looks as if she
were prepared to bury them, and not indiposed to
enjoy the ceremony. Even Kitty Collins has
caught the contagious gloom, as I perceive when
she brings in the coffee-urn — a solemn and sculp-
turesque urn at any time, but monumental now —
and sets it down in front of Miss Abigail. Miss
Abigail gazes at the urn as if it held the ashes of
her ancestors, instead of a generous quantity of fine
old Java coffee. The meal progresses in silence.

Our parlor is by no means thrown open every
day. It is open this
June morning, and is
pervaded by a strong
smell of centre-table.
The furniture of the
room, and the little
China ornaments on
the mantel-piece, have
a constrained, unfamil-
liar look. My grand-
father sits in a ma-
hogany chair, reading
a large Bible covered
with green baize. Miss

Crushed

Abigail occupies one end of the sofa, and has her
hands crossed stiffly in her lap. I sit in the corner,

crushed. Robinson Crusoe and Gil Blas are in close confinement. Baron Trenck, who managed to escape from the fortress of Glatz, can't for the life of him get out of our sitting-room closet. Even the Rivermouth Barnacle is suppressed until Monday. Genial converse, harmless books, smiles, lightsome hearts, all are banished. If I want to read anything, I can read Baxter's Saints' Rest. I would die first. So I sit there kicking my heels, thinking about New Orleans, and watching a morbid blue-bottle fly that attempts to commit suicide by butting his head against the window-pane. Listen! — no, yes — it is — it is the robins singing in the garden — the grateful, joyous robins singing away like mad, just as if it were not Sunday. Their audacity tickles me.

My grandfather looks up, and inquires in a sepulchral voice if I am ready for Sabbath-school. It is time to go. I like the Sabbath-school; there are bright young faces *there*, at all events. When I get out into the sunshine alone, I draw a long breath; I would turn a somersault up against Neighbor Penhallow's newly painted fence if I had not my best trousers on, so glad am I to escape from the oppressive atmosphere of the Nutter House.

Sabbath-school over, I go to meeting, joining my grandfather, who does not appear to be any relation to me this day, and Miss Abigail, in the porch. Our minister holds out very little hope to any of us of being saved. Convinced that I am a lost creature, in common with the human family, I return home behind my guardians at a snail's pace. We have a dead-cold dinner. I saw it laid out yesterday.

There is a long interval between this repast and the second service, and a still longer interval between the beginning and the end of that service ; for the Rev. Wibird Hawkins's sermons are none of the shortest, whatever else they may be.

After meeting, my grandfather and I take a walk. We visit, appropriately enough, a neighboring graveyard. I am by this time in a condition of mind to become a willing inmate of the place. The usual evening prayer-meeting is postponed for some reason. At half past eight I go to bed.

This is the way Sunday was observed in the Nutter House, and pretty generally throughout the town, twenty years ago. People who were prosperous and natural and happy on Saturday became the most rueful of human beings in the brief space of twelve hours. I do not think there was any hypocrisy in this. It was merely the old Puritan austerity cropping out once a week. Many of these people were pure Christians every day in the seven — excepting the seventh. Then they were decorous and solemn to the verge of moroseness. I should not like to be misunderstood on this point. Sunday is a blessed day, and therefore it should not be made a gloomy one. It is

the Lord's day, and I do believe that cheerful
hearts and faces are not unpleasant in His sight.

"O day of rest? How beautiful, how fair,
How welcome to the weary and the old!
Day of the Lord! and truce to earthly cares!
Day of the Lord, as all our days should be!
Ah, why will man by his austerities
Shut out the blessed sunshine and the light,
And make of thee a dungeon of despair !"

CHAPTER VII

ONE MEMORABLE NIGHT

Two months had elapsed since my arrival at Rivermouth, when the approach of an important celebration produced the greatest excitement among the juvenile population of the town.

There was very little hard study done in the Temple Grammar School the week preceding the Fourth of July. For my part, my heart and brain were so full of fire-crackers, Roman-candles, rockets, pin-wheels, squibs, and gunpowder in various seductive forms, that I wonder I did not explode under Mr. Grimshaw's very nose. I could not do a sum to save me; I could not tell, for love or money, whether Tallahassee was the capital of Tennessee or of Florida; the present and the pluperfect tenses were inextricably mixed in my memory, and I did not know a verb from an adjective when I met one. This was not alone my condition, but that of every boy in the school.

Mr. Grimshaw considerately made allowances for our temporary distraction, and sought to fix our interest on the lessons by connecting them directly or indirectly with the coming Event. The class in arithmetic, for instance, was requested to state how many boxes of fire-crackers, each box measuring sixteen inches square, could be stored in a room of such and such dimensions. He gave us the Declaration of Independence for a parsing exercise, and in geography confined his questions almost exclusively to localities rendered famous in the Revolutionary War. " What did the people of Boston do with the tea on board the English vessels ? " asked our wily instructor.

" Threw it into the river ! " shrieked the smaller boys, with an impetuosity that made Mr. Grimshaw smile in spite of himself. One luckless urchin said, " Chucked it," for which happy expression he was kept in at recess.

Notwithstanding these clever stratagems, there was not much solid work done by anybody. The trail of the serpent (an inexpensive but dangerous fire-toy) was over us all. We went round deformed by quantities of Chinese crackers artlessly concealed in our trousers-pockets ; and if a boy whipped out his handkerchief without proper precaution, he was sure to let off two or three torpedoes.

Even Mr. Grimshaw was made a sort of accessory to the universal demoralization. In calling the school to order, he always rapped on the table with a heavy ruler.   Under the green baize table-cloth, on the exact spot where he usually struck, a certain boy, whose name I withhold, placed a fat torpedo. The result was a loud explosion, which caused Mr. Grimshaw to look queer. Charley

Marden was at the water-pail, at the time, and directed general attention to himself by strangling for several seconds and then squirting a slender thread of water over the blackboard.

Mr. Grimshaw fixed his eyes reproachfully on Charley, but said nothing. The real culprit (it was not Charley Marden, but the boy whose name I withhold) instantly regretted his badness, and after school confessed the whole thing to Mr. Grimshaw, who heaped coals of fire upon the nameless boy's head by giving him five cents for the Fourth of July. If

Mr. 'Grimshaw looked Queer

Mr. Grimshaw had caned this unknown youth, the punishment would not have been half so severe.

On the last day of June the Captain received a letter from my father, inclosing five dollars "for my son Tom," which enabled that young gentleman to make regal preparations for the celebration of our national independence. A portion of this money, two dollars, I hastened to invest in fireworks; the balance I put by for contingencies. In placing the fund in my possession, the Captain imposed one condition that dampened my ardor

considerably — I was to buy no gunpowder. I
might have all the snapping-crackers and torpedoes I wanted; but gunpowder was out of the
question.

I thought this rather hard, for all my young
friends were provided with pistols of various sizes.
Pepper Whitcomb had a horse-pistol nearly as
large as himself, and Jack Harris, though he, to
be sure, was a big boy, was going to have a real
old-fashioned flint-lock musket. However, I did
not mean to let this drawback destroy my happiness. I had one charge of powder stowed away
in the little brass pistol which I brought from
New Orleans, and was bound to make a noise in
the world once, if I never did again.

It was a custom observed from time immemo-
rial for the towns-boys to have a bonfire on the
Square on the midnight before the Fourth. I did
not ask the Captain's leave to attend this ceremony, for I had a general idea that he would not
give it. If the Captain, I reasoned, does not forbid
me, I break no orders by going. Now this was a
specious line of argument, and the mishaps that
befell me in consequence of adopting it were richly
deserved.

On the evening of the third I retired to bed very
early, in order to disarm suspicion. I did not
sleep a wink, waiting for eleven o'clock to come
round ; and I thought it never would come round,
as I lay counting from time to time the slow

strokes of the ponderous bell in the steeple of the
Old North Church. At length the laggard hour
arrived. While the clock was striking I jumped
out of bed and began dressing.

My grandfather and Miss Abigail were heavy
sleepers, and I might have stolen downstairs and
out at the front door undetected ; but such a com-
monplace proceeding did not suit my adventurous
disposition. I fastened one end of a rope (it was
a few yards cut from Kitty Collins's clothes-line)
to the bedpost nearest the window, and cautiously
climbed out on the wide pediment over the hall
door. I had neglected to knot the rope ; the result was, that, the moment I swung clear of the
pediment, I descended like a flash of lightning,
and warmed both my hands smartly. The rope,
moreover, was four or five feet too short ; so I got
a fall that would have proved. serious had I not
tumbled into the middle of one of the big rosebushes growing on either side of the steps.

I scrambled out of that without delay, and was
congratulating myself on my good luck, when I
saw by the light of the setting moon the form of
a man leaning over the garden gate. It was one
of the town watch, who had probably been observing my operations with curiosity. Seeing no
chance of escape, I put a bold face on the matter
and walked directly up to him.

"What on airth air you a-doin'?" asked the
man, grasping the collar of my jacket.

"I live here, sir, if you please," I replied, "and am going to the bonfire. I did n't want to wake up the old folks, that 's all."

The man cocked his eye at me in the most amiable manner, and released his hold.

"Boys is boys," he muttered. He did not attempt to stop me as I slipped through the gate.

Once beyond his clutches, I took to my heels and soon reached the Square, where I found forty or fifty fellows assembled, engaged in building a pyramid of tar-barrels. The palms of my hands still tingled so that I could not join in the sport. I stood in the doorway of the Nautilus Bank, watching the workers, among whom I recognized lots of my schoolmates. They looked like a legion of imps, coming and going in the twilight, busy in raising some infernal edifice. What a Babel of voices it was, everybody directing everybody else, and everybody doing everything wrong !

When all was prepared, some one applied a match to the sombre pile. A fiery tongue thrust itself out here and there, then suddenly the whole fabric burst into flames, blazing and crackling beautifully. This was a signal for the boys to join hands and dance around the burning barrels, which they did, shouting like mad creatures. When the fire had burnt down a little, fresh staves were brought and heaped on the pyre. In the excitement of the moment I forgot my tingling palms, and found myself in the thick of the carousal.

Before we were half ready, our combustible material was expended, and a disheartening kind of darkness settled down upon us. The boys collected together here and there in knots, consulting as to what should be done. It yet lacked four or five hours of daybreak, and none of us were in the humor to return to bed. I approached one of the groups standing near the town-pump, and discovered in the uncertain light of the dying brands the figures of Jack Harris, Phil Adams, Harry Blake, and Pepper Whitcomb, their faces streaked with perspiration and tar, and their whole appearance suggestive of New Zealand chiefs.

"Hullo! here's Tom Bailey!" shouted Pepper Whitcomb; "he'll join in!"

Of course he would. The sting had gone out of my hands, and I was ripe for anything — none the less ripe for not knowing what was on the *tapis*. After whispering together for a moment, the boys motioned me to follow them.

We glided out from the crowd and silently wended our way through a neighboring alley, at the head of which stood a tumble-down old barn, owned by one Ezra Wingate. In former days this was the stable of the mail-coach that ran between Rivermouth and Boston. When the railroad superseded that primitive mode of travel, the lumbering vehicle was rolled into the barn, and there it stayed. The stage-driver, after prophesying the immediate downfall of the nation, died of grief and apoplexy, and the old coach followed in his wake as fast as it could by quietly dropping to pieces. The barn had the reputation of being haunted, and I think we all kept very close together when we found ourselves standing in the black shadow cast by the tall gable. Here, in a low voice, Jack Harris laid bare his plan, which was to burn the ancient stage-coach.

"The old trundle-cart is n't worth twenty-five cents," said Jack Harris, "and Ezra Wingate ought to thank us for getting the rubbish out of the way. But if any fellow here does n't want to have a hand in it, let him cut and run, and keep a quiet tongue in his head ever after."

With this he pulled out the staples that held the rusty padlock, and the big barn door swung slowly open. The interior of the stable was pitch-dark, of course. As we made a movement to enter, a sudden scrambling, and the sound of heavy bodies leaping in all directions, caused us to start back in terror.

"Rats!" cried Phil Adams.

"Bats!" exclaimed Harry Blake.

"Cats!" suggested Jack Harris. "Who's afraid?"

Well, the truth is, we were all afraid; and if the pole of the stage had not been lying close to the threshold, I do not believe anything on earth would have induced us to cross it. We seized hold of the pole-straps and succeeded with great trouble in dragging the coach out. The two fore wheels had rusted to the axle-tree, and refused to revolve. It was the merest skeleton of a coach. The cushions had long since been removed, and the leather hangings, where they had not crumbled away, dangled in shreds from the worm-eaten frame. A load of ghosts and a span of phantom horses to drag them would have made the ghastly thing complete.

Luckily for our undertaking, the stable stood at the top of a very steep hill. With three boys to push behind, and two in front to steer, we started the old coach on its last trip with little or no difficulty. Our speed increased every moment, and, the fore wheels becoming unlocked as we arrived at the foot of the declivity, we charged upon the crowd like a regiment of cavalry, scattering the people right and left. Before reaching the bonfire, to which some one had added several bushels of shavings, Jack Harris and Phil Adams, who were steering, dropped on the ground, and allowed the vehicle to pass over them, which it did without injuring them; but the boys who were clinging for dear life to the trunk-rack behind fell over the prostrate steersmen, and there we all lay in a heap, two or three of us quite picturesque with the nose-bleed.

The coach, with an intuitive perception of what was expected of it, plunged into the centre of the kindling shavings, and stopped. The flames sprung up and clung to the rotten woodwork, which burned like tinder. At this moment a figure was seen leaping wildly from the inside of the blazing coach. The figure made three bounds towards us, and tripped over Harry Blake. It was Pepper Whitcomb, with his hair somewhat singed, and his eyebrows completely scorched off!

Pepper had slyly ensconced himself on the back seat before we started, intending to have a neat little ride down hill, and a laugh at us afterwards. But the laugh, as it happened, was on our side, or would have been, if half a dozen watchmen had not suddenly pounced down upon us, as we lay scrambling on the ground, weak with mirth over Pepper's misfortune. We were collared and marched off before we well knew what had happened.

The abrupt transition from the noise and light of the Square to the silent, gloomy brick room in the rear of the Meat Market seemed like the work of enchantment. We stared at each other aghast.

" Well," remarked Jack Harris, with a sickly smile, "this *is* a go!"

" No go, I should say," whimpered Harry Blake, glancing at the bare brick walls and the heavy iron-plated door.

" Never say die," muttered Phil Adams, dolefully.

The bridewell was a small low-studded chamber built up against the rear end of the Meat Market, and approached from the Square by a narrow passageway. A portion of the room was partitioned

The Interrupted Celebration

off into eight cells, numbered, each capable of holding two persons. The cells were full at the time,
as we presently discovered by seeing several hid-
eous faces leering out at us through the gratings
of the doors.

A smoky oil-lamp in a lantern suspended from
the ceiling threw a flickering light over the apartment, which contained no furniture excepting a
couple of stout wooden benches. It was a dismal
place by night, and only little less dismal by day,
for the tall houses surrounding "the lock-up" prevented the faintest ray of sunshine from penetrat-
ing the ventilator over the door — a long narrow
window opening inward and propped up by a piece
of lath.

As we seated ourselves in a row on one of the
benches, I imagine that our aspect was anything
but cheerful. Adams and Harris looked very anxious, and Harry Blake, whose nose had just stopped
bleeding, was mournfully carving his name, by sheer
force of habit, on the prison bench. I do not think
I ever saw a more "wrecked" expression on any
human countenance than Pepper Whitcomb's presented. His look of natural astonishment at finding himself incarcerated in a jail was considerably
heightened by his lack of eyebrows.

As for me, it was only by thinking how the late
Baron Trenck would have conducted himself under
similar circumstances that I was able to restrain
my tears.

None of us were inclined to conversation. A deep silence, broken now and then by a startling snore from the cells, reigned throughout the chamber. By and by Pepper Whitcomb glanced nervously towards Phil Adams and said, "Phil, do you think they will — *hang us?*"

"Hang your grandmother!" returned Adams, impatiently; "what I 'm afraid of is that they 'll keep us locked up until the Fourth is over."

"You ain't smart ef they do!" cried a voice from one of the cells. It was a deep bass voice that sent a chill through me.

"Who are you?" said Jack Harris, addressing the cells in general; for the echoing qualities of the room made it difficult to locate the voice.

"That don't matter," replied the speaker, putting his face close up to the gratings of No. 3, "but ef I was a youngster like you, free an' easy outside there, this spot would n't hold *me* long."

"That 's so!" chimed several of the prison-birds, wagging their heads behind the iron lattices.

"Hush!" whispered Jack Harris, rising from his seat and walking on tip-toe to the door of cell No. 3. "What would you do?"

"Do? Why, I 'd pile them 'ere benches up agin that 'ere door, an' crawl out of that 'ere winder in no time. That 's my adwice."

"And werry good adwice it is, Jim," said the occupant of No. 5 approvingly.

Jack Harris seemed to be of the same opinion, for he hastily placed the benches one on the top of another under the ventilator, and, climbing up on the highest bench, peeped out into the passageway.

"If any gent happens to have a nine-pence about him," said the man in cell No. 3, "there's a sufferin' family here as could make use of it. Smallest favors gratefully received, an' no questions axed."

This appeal touched a new silver quarter of a dollar in my trousers-pocket; I fished out the coin from a mass of fireworks, and gave it to the prisoner.

"*What would you do?*"

He appeared to be so good-natured a fellow that I ventured to ask what he had done to get into jail.

"Intirely innocent. I was clapped in here by a rascally nevew as wishes to enjoy my wealth afore I'm dead."

"Your name, sir?" I inquired, with a view of

reporting the outrage to my grandfather and having the injured person reinstated in society.

"Git out, you insolent young reptyle!" shouted the man, in a passion.

I retreated precipitately, amid a roar of laughter from the other cells.

"Can't you keep still?" exclaimed Harris, withdrawing his head from the window.

A portly watchman usually sat on a stool outside the door day and night; but on this particular occasion, his services being required elsewhere, the bridewell had been left to guard itself.

"All clear," whispered Jack Harris, as he vanished through the aperture and dropped softly on the ground outside. We all followed him expeditiously — Pepper Whitcomb and myself getting stuck in the window for a moment in our frantic efforts not to be last.

"Now, boys, everybody for himself!"

CHAPTER VIII

THE ADVENTURES OF A FOURTH

THE sun cast a broad column of quivering gold across the river at the foot of our street, just as I reached the doorstep of the Nutter House. Kitty Collins, with her dress tucked about her so that she looked as if she had on a pair of calico trousers, was washing off the sidewalk.

"Arrah, you bad boy!" cried Kitty, leaning on the mop-handle, "the Capen has jist been askin' for you. He's gone up town, now. It's a nate thing you done with my clothes-line, and it's me you may thank for gettin' it out of the way before the Capen come down."

The kind creature had hauled in the rope, and my escapade had not been discovered by the family; but I knew very well that the burning of the stage-coach, and the arrest of the boys concerned in the mischief, were sure to reach my grandfather's ears sooner or later.

"Well, Thomas," said the old gentleman, an hour or so afterwards, beaming upon me benevolently across the breakfast-table, "you did n't wait to be called this morning."

"No, sir," I replied, growing very warm, "I

took a little run up town to see what was going on."

I did not say anything about the little run I took home again!

"They had quite a time on the Square last night," remarked Captain Nutter, looking up from the Rivermouth Barnacle, which was always placed beside his coffee-cup at breakfast.

I felt that my hair was preparing to stand on end.

"Quite a time," continued my grandfather. "Some boys broke into Ezra Wingate's barn and carried off the old stage-coach. The young rascals! I do believe they 'd burn up the whole town if they had their way."

With this he resumed the paper. After a long silence he exclaimed, "Hullo!" — upon which I nearly fell off the chair.

"'Miscreants unknown,'" read my grandfather, following the paragraph with his forefinger; "'escaped from the bridewell, leaving no clew to their identity, except the letter H, cut on one of the benches.' 'Five dollars reward offered for the apprehension of the perpetrators.' Sho! I hope Wingate will catch them."

" *Miscreants unknown* "

trators.' Sho! I hope Wingate will catch them."

I do not see how I continued to live, for on hearing this the breath went entirely out of my body.

I beat a retreat from the room as soon as I could, and flew to the stable with a misty intention of mounting Gypsy and escaping from the place. I was pondering what steps to take, when Jack Harris and Charley Marden entered the yard.

"I say," said Harris as blithe as a lark, " has old Wingate been here?"

"Been here?" I cried, "I should hope not!"

"The whole thing's out, you know," said Harris, pulling Gypsy's forelock over her eyes and blowing playfully into her nostrils.

"You don't mean it!" I gasped.

"Yes, I do, and we are to pay Wingate three dollars apiece. He'll make rather a good spec out of it."

"But how did he discover that we were the — the miscreants?" I asked, quoting mechanically from the Rivermouth Barnacle.

"Why, he saw us take the old ark, confound him! He's been trying to sell it any time these ten years. Now he has sold it to us. When he found that we had slipped out of the Meat Market, he went right off and wrote the advertisement offering five dollars reward; though he knew well enough who had taken the coach, for he came round to my father's house before the paper was printed to talk the matter over. Was n't the governor mad, though! But it's all settled, I tell you. We're to pay Wingate fifteen dollars for the old go-cart, which he wanted to sell the other day for seventy-five cents, and could n't. It's a down-right swindle. But the funny part of it is to come."

"Oh, there's a funny part to it, is there?" I remarked bitterly.

"Yes. The moment Bill Conway saw the adver-tisement, he knew it was Harry Blake who cut that letter H on the bench ; so off he rushes up to Win-gate — kind of him, was n't it ? — and claims the reward. 'Too late, young man,' says old Wingate, 'the culprits has been discovered.' You see Sly-boots had n't any intention of paying that five dol-lars."

Jack Harris's statement lifted a weight from my bosom. The article in the Rivermouth Barna-cle had placed the affair before me in a new light. I had thoughtlessly committed a grave offense. Though the property in question was valueless, we were clearly wrong in destroying it. At the same time, Mr. Wingate *had* tacitly sanctioned the act by not preventing it when he might easily have done so. He had allowed his property to be destroyed in order that he might realize a large profit.

Without waiting to hear more, I went straight to Captain Nutter, and, laying my remaining three dollars on his knee, confessed my share in the pre-vious night's transaction.

The Captain heard me through in profound silence, pocketed the bank-notes, and walked off without speaking a word. He had punished me in his own whimsical fashion at the breakfast-table, for, at the

very moment he was harrowing up my soul by reading the extracts from the Rivermouth Barnacle, he
not only knew all about the bonfire, but had paid
Ezra Wingate his three dollars.   Such was the du-
plicity of that aged impostor !

I think Captain Nutter was justified in retaining
my pocket-money, as additional punishment, though
the possession of it later in the day would have got
me out of a difficult position, as the reader will see
farther on.

I returned with a light heart and a large piece of
punk to my friends in the stable-yard, where we celebrated the termination of our trouble by setting off
two packs of fire-crackers in an empty wine-cask.
They made a prodigious racket, but failed somehow
to fully express my feelings.   The little brass pistol
in my bedroom suddenly occurred to me.   It had
been loaded I do not know how many months, long
before I left New Orleans, and now was the time,
if ever, to fire it off.   Muskets, blunderbusses, and
pistols were banging away lively all over town,
and the smell of gunpowder, floating on the air, set
me wild to add something respectable to the universal din.

When the pistol was produced, Jack Harris examined the rusty cap and prophesied that it would
not explode.

"Never mind," said I, "let 's try it."

I had fired the pistol once, secretly, in New Orleans, and, remembering the noise it gave birth to

on that occasion, I shut both eyes tight as I pulled
the trigger.   The hammer clicked on the cap with
a dull, dead sound.   Then Harris tried it ; then
Charley Marden ; then I took it again, and after
three or four trials was on the point of giving it

" Are you hurt ?"

up as a bad job, when the obstinate thing went off
with a tremendous explosion, nearly jerking my arm
from the socket.   The smoke cleared away, and
there I stood with the stock of the pistol clutched
convulsively in my hand — the barrel, lock, trigger,
and ramrod having vanished into thin air.

   "Are you hurt?" cried the boys in one breath.

" N—no," I replied, dubiously, for the concussion had bewildered me a little.

When I realized the nature of the calamity, my grief was excessive. I cannot imagine what led me to do so ridiculous a thing, but I gravely buried the remains of my beloved pistol in our back garden, and erected over the mound a slate tablet to the effect that " Mr. Barker, formerly of New Orleans, was Killed accidently on the Fourth of july, 18— in the 2d year of his Age."[1] Binny Wallace, arriving on the spot just after the disaster, and Charley Marden (who enjoyed the obsequies immensely), acted with me as chief mourners. I, for my part, was a very sincere one.

As I turned away in a disconsolate mood from the garden, Charley Marden remarked that he should not be surprised if the pistol-but took root and grew into a mahogany-tree or something. He said he once planted an old musket-stock, and shortly afterwards a lot of *shoots* sprung up ! Jack Harris laughed ; but neither I nor Binny Wallace saw Charley's wicked joke.

We were now joined by Pepper Whitcomb, Fred Langdon, and several other desperate characters, on their way to the Square, which was always a busy place when public festivities were going on. Feeling that I was still in disgrace with the Cap-

[1] This inscription is copied from a triangular-shaped piece of slate, still preserved in the garret of the Nutter House, together with the pistol-but itself, which was subsequently dug up for a *post-mortem* examination.

tain, I thought it politic to ask his consent before accompanying the boys.

He gave it with some hesitation, advising me to be careful not to get in front of the firearms. Once he put his fingers mechanically into his vest-pocket and half drew forth some dollar-bills, then slowly thrust them back again as his sense of justice overcame his genial disposition. I guess it cut the old gentleman to the heart to be obliged to keep me out of my pocket-money. I know it did me. However, as I was passing through the hall, Miss Abigail, with a very severe cast of countenance, slipped a brand-new quarter into my hand. We had silver currency in those days, thank Heaven!

Great were the bustle and confusion on the Square. By the way, I don't know why they called this large open space a square, unless because it was an oval — an oval formed by the confluence of half a dozen streets, now thronged by crowds of smartly dressed towns-people and country folks ; for Rivermouth on the Fourth was the centre of attraction to the inhabitants of the neighboring villages.

On one side of the Square were twenty or thirty booths arranged in a semicircle, gay with little flags and seductive with lemonade, ginger-beer, and seed cakes. Here and there were tables at which could be purchased the smaller sort of fireworks, such as pin-wheels, serpents, double-headers, and punk warranted not to go out. Many of the adjacent houses made a pretty display of bunting, and across each of the streets opening on the Square was an arch of spruce and evergreen, blossoming all over with patriotic mottoes and paper roses.

It was a noisy, merry, bewildering scene as we came upon the ground. The incessant rattle of small arms, the booming of the twelve-pounder firing on the Mill Dam, and the silvery clangor of the church-bells ringing simultaneously — not to mention an ambitious brass-band that was blowing itself to pieces on a balcony — were enough to drive one distracted. We amused ourselves for an hour or two, darting in and out among the crowd and setting off our crackers. At one o'clock the Hon. Hezekiah Elkins mounted a platform in the middle of the Square and delivered an oration, to which his "feller-citizens" did not pay much attention, having all they could do to dodge the squibs that were set loose upon them by mischievous boys stationed on the surrounding housetops.

Our little party, which had picked up recruits here and there, not being swayed by eloquence, withdrew to a booth on the outskirts of the crowd, where we regaled ourselves with root beer at two cents a glass. I recollect being much struck by the placard surmounting this tent :

ROOT BEER
SOLD HERE.

It seemed to me the perfection of pith and poetry.

What could be more terse? Not a word to spare, and yet everything fully expressed. Rhyme and rhythm faultless. It was a delightful poet who made those verses. As for the beer itself — that, I think, must have made from the root of all evil!

The Perfection of Pith and Poetry

A single glass of it insured an uninterrupted pain for twenty-four hours.

The influence of my liberality working on Charley Marden — for it was I who paid for the beer — he presently invited us all to take an ice-cream with him at Pettingil's saloon. Pettingil was the Delmonico of Rivermouth. He furnished ices and confectionery for aristocratic balls and parties, and did not disdain to officiate as leader of the orchestra at the same; for Pettingil played on the violin, as Pepper Whitcomb described it, " like Old Scratch."

Pettingil's confectionery store was on the corner of Willow and High streets. The saloon, separated from the shop by a flight of three steps leading to a door hung with faded red drapery, had about it an air of mystery and seclusion quite delightful. Four windows, also draped, faced the side - street, affording an unobstructed view of Marm Hatch's back yard, where a number of inexplicable garments on a clothes-line were always to be seen careering in the wind.

There was a lull just then in the ice-cream business, it being dinner-time, and we found the saloon unoccupied. When we had seated ourselves around the largest marble-topped table, Charley Marden in a manly voice ordered twelve sixpenny ice-creams, "strawberry and verneller mixed."

It was a magnificent sight, those twelve chilly glasses entering the room on a waiter, the red and white custard rising from each glass like a church-steeple, and the spoon-handle shooting up from the apex like a spire. I doubt if a person of the nicest palate could have distinguished, with his eyes shut, which was the vanilla and which the strawberry: but if I could at this moment obtain a cream tasting as that did, I would give five dollars for a very small quantity.

We fell to with a will, and so evenly balanced were our capabilities that we finished our creams together, the spoons clinking in the glasses like one spoon.

"Let's have some more!" cried Charley Marden, with the air of Aladdin ordering up a fresh hogshead of pearls and rubies. "Tom Bailey, tell Pettingil to send in another round."

Could I credit my ears? I looked at him to see if he were in earnest. He meant it. In a moment more I was leaning over the counter giving directions for a second supply. Thinking it would make

no difference to such a gorgeous young sybarite as
Marden, I took the liberty of ordering ninepenny
creams this time.

On returning to the saloon, what was my horror
at finding it empty!

There were the twelve cloudy glasses, standing
in a circle on the sticky marble slab, and not a boy
to be seen.   A pair of hands letting go their hold
on the window-sill outside explained matters.   I
had been made a victim.

I couldn't stay and face Pettingil, whose pep-
pery temper was well known among the boys.   I
had not a cent in the world to appease him.   What
should I do?   I heard the clink of approaching
glasses — the ninepenny creams.   I rushed to the
nearest window.   It was only five feet to the
ground.   I threw myself out as if I had been an
old hat.

Landing on my feet, I fled breathlessly down
High Street, through Willow, and was turning into
Brierwood Place when the sound of several voices,
calling to me in distress, stopped my progress.

"Look out, you fool! the mine! the mine!"
yelled the warning voices.

Several men and boys were standing at the head
of the street, making insane gestures to me to
avoid something.   But I saw no mine, only in the
middle of the road in front of me was a common
flour-barrel, which, as I gazed at it, suddenly rose
into the air with a terrific explosion.   I felt myself

thrown violently off my feet.   I remember nothing else, excepting that, as I went up, I caught a momentary glimpse of Ezra Wingate leering through his shop window like an avenging spirit.

The mine that had wrought me woe was not properly a mine at all, but merely a few ounces of powder placed under an empty keg or barrel and fired with a slow-match.   Boys who did not happen to

The Result of the Explosion

have pistols or cannon generally burnt their powder in this fashion.

For an account of what followed I am indebted to hearsay, for I was insensible when the bystanders picked me up and carried me home on a shutter borrowed from the proprietor of Pettingil's saloon. I was supposed to be killed, but happily (happily for me at least) I was merely stunned.   I lay in a semi-unconscious state until eight o'clock that night, when I attempted to speak. Miss Abigail, who watched by the bedside, put her ear down to my lips and was saluted with these remarkable words :

"Strawberry and verneller mixed!"

"Mercy on us! what is the boy saying?" cried Miss Abigail.

"Rootbeersoldhere!"

CHAPTER IX

I BECOME AN R. M. C.

In the course of ten days I recovered sufficiently from my injuries to attend school, where, for a little while, I was looked upon as a hero, on account of having been blown up. What do we not make a hero of? The distraction which prevailed in the classes the week preceding the Fourth had subsided, and nothing remained to indicate the recent festivities, excepting a noticeable want of eyebrows on the part of Pepper Whitcomb and myself.

In August we had two weeks' vacation. It was about this time that I became a member of the Rivermouth Centipedes, a secret society composed of twelve of the Temple Grammar School boys. This was an honor to which I had long aspired, but, being a new boy, I was not admitted to the fraternity until my character had fully developed itself.

It was a very select society, the object of which I never fathomed, though I was an active member of the body during the remainder of my residence at Rivermouth, and at one time held the onerous position of F. C. — First Centipede. Each of the elect wore a copper cent (some occult association being established between a cent apiece and a centipede!) suspended by a string round his neck. The medals were worn next the skin, and it was while bathing one day at Grave Point, with Jack Harris and Fred Langdon, that I had my curiosity roused to the highest pitch by a sight of these singular emblems. As soon as I ascertained the existence of a boys' club, of course I was ready to die to join it. And eventually I was allowed to join.

The initiation ceremony took place in Fred Langdon's barn, where I was submitted to a series of trials not calculated to soothe the nerves of a timorous boy. Before being led to the Grotto of Enchantment — such was the modest title given to the loft over my friend's wood-house — my hands were securely pinioned, and my eyes covered with a thick silk handkerchief. At the head of the stairs I was told in an unrecognizable, husky voice, that it was not yet too late to retreat if I felt myself physically too weak to undergo the necessary tortures. I replied that I was not too weak, in a tone which I intended to be resolute, but which, in spite of me, seemed to come from the pit of my stomach.

"It is well!" said the husky voice.

I did not feel so sure about that ; but, having made up my mind to be a Centipede, a Centipede I was bound to be. Other boys had passed through the ordeal and lived, why should not I ?

A prolonged silence followed this preliminary examination, and I was wondering what would come next, when a pistol fired off close by my ear deafened me for a moment. The unknown voice then directed me to take ten steps forward and stop at the word halt. I took ten steps, and halted.

" Stricken mortal," said a second husk voice, more husky, if possible, than the first, "if you had advanced another inch, you would have disappeared down an abyss three thousand feet deep ! "

I naturally shrunk back at this friendly piece of information. A prick from some two-pronged instrument, evidently a pitchfork, gently checked my retreat. I was then conducted to the brink of several other precipices, and ordered to step over many dangerous chasms, where the result would have been instant death if I had committed the least mistake. I have neglected to say that my movements were accompanied by dismal groans from different parts of the grotto.

Gently checked

Finally, I was led up a steep plank to what appeared to me an incalculable height. Here I stood breathless while the by-laws were read aloud. A more extraordinary code of laws never came from the brain of man. The penalties attached to the abject being who should reveal any of the secrets of the society were enough to make the blood run cold. A second pistol-shot was heard, the something I stood on sunk with a crash beneath my feet, and I fell two miles, as nearly as I could compute it. At the same instant the handkerchief was whisked from my eyes, and I found myself standing in an empty hogshead surrounded by twelve masked figures fantastically dressed. One of the conspirators was really appalling with a tin sauce-pan on his head, and a tiger-skin sleigh-robe thrown over his shoulders. I scarcely need say that there were no vestiges to be seen of the fearful gulfs over which I had passed so cautiously. My ascent had been to the top of the hogshead, and my descent to the bottom thereof. Holding one another by the hand, and chanting a low dirge, the Mystic Twelve revolved about me. This concluded the ceremony. With a merry shout the boys threw off their masks, and I was declared a regularly installed member of the R. M. C.

I afterwards had a good deal of sport out of the club, for these initiations, as you may imagine, were sometimes very comical spectacles, especially when the aspirant for centipedal honors happened to be of a timid disposition. If he showed the slightest terror, he was certain to be tricked unmercifully. One of our subsequent devices — a humble invention of my own — was to request the blindfolded

The Initiation

candidate to put out his tongue, whereupon the
First Centipede would say, in a low tone, as if not
intended for the ear of the victim, "Diabolus,
fetch me the red-hot iron!" The expedition with
which that tongue would disappear was simply ridiculous.

Our meetings were held in various barns, at no
stated periods, but as circumstances suggested.
Any member had a right to call a meeting. Each
boy who failed to report himself was fined one cent.
Whenever a member had reasons for thinking that
another member would be unable to attend, he
called a meeting. For instance, immediately on
learning the death of Harry Blake's great-grand-
father, I issued a call. By these simple and ingenious measures we kept our treasury in a flourish-
ing condition, sometimes having on hand as much
as a dollar and a quarter.

I have said that the society had no especial object. It is true, there was a tacit understanding
among us that the Centipedes were to stand by one
another on all occasions, though I don't remember
that they did; but further than this we had no
purpose, unless it was to accomplish as a body the
same amount of mischief which we were sure to
do as individuals. To mystify the staid and slow-
going Rivermouthians was our frequent pleasure.
Several of our pranks won us such a reputation
among the townsfolk that we were credited with
having a large finger in whatever went amiss in
the place.

One morning, about a week after my admission into the secret order, the quiet citizens awoke to find that the sign-boards of all the principal streets had changed places during the night. People who went trustfully to sleep in Currant Square opened their eyes in Honeysuckle Terrace. Jones's Avenue at the north end had suddenly become Walnut Street, and Peanut Street was nowhere to be found. Confusion reigned. The town authorities took the matter in hand without delay, and six of the Temple Grammar School boys were summoned to appear before Justice Clapham.

Having tearfully disclaimed to my grandfather all knowledge of the transaction, I disappeared from the family circle, and was not apprehended until late in the afternoon, when the Captain dragged me ignominiously from the haymow and conducted me, more dead than alive, to the office of Justice Clapham. Here I encountered five other pallid culprits, who had been fished out of divers coal-bins, garrets, and chicken-coops, to answer the demands of the outraged laws. (Charley Marden had hidden himself in a pile of gravel behind his father's house, and looked like a recently exhumed mummy.)

There was not the least evidence against us; and indeed we were wholly innocent of the offense. The trick, as was afterwards proved, had been played by a party of soldiers stationed at the fort in the harbor. We were indebted for our arrest

to Master Conway, who had slyly dropped a hint,
within the hearing of Selectman Mudge, to the
effect that "young Bailey and his five cronies
could tell something about them signs." When he
was called upon to make good his assertion, he was

Charley Marden exhumed

considerably more terrified than the Centipedes,
though *they* were ready to sink into their shoes.

At our next meeting it was unanimously resolved
that Conway's animosity should not be quietly submitted to. He had sought to inform against us in
the stage-coach business; he had volunteered to
carry Pettingil's "little bill" for twenty-four ice-
creams to Charley Marden's father; and now he
had caused us to be arraigned before Justice Clap-

ham on a charge equally groundless and painful. After much noisy discussion a plan of retaliation was agreed upon.

There was a certain slim, mild apothecary in the town, by the name of Meeks. It was generally given out that Mr. Meeks had a vague desire to get married, but, being a shy and timorous youth, lacked the moral courage to do so. It was also well known that the Widow Conway had not buried her heart with the late lamented. As to her shyness, that was not so clear. Indeed, her attentions to Mr. Meeks, whose mother she might have been, were of a nature not to be misunderstood, and were not misunderstood by any one but Mr. Meeks himself.

The widow carried on a dressmaking establishment at her residence on the corner opposite Meeks's drug-store, and kept a wary eye on all the young ladies from Miss Dorothy Gibbs's Female Institute who patronized the shop for soda-water, acid-drops, and slate-pencils. In the afternoon the widow was usually seen seated, smartly dressed, at her window upstairs, casting destructive glances across the street — the artificial roses in her cap and her whole languishing manner saying as plainly as a label on a prescription, " To be Taken Immediately!"   But Mr. Meeks did n't take.

The lady's fondness and the gentleman's blindness were topics ably handled at every sewing-circle in the town.   It was through these two luckless individuals that we proposed to strike a blow at the common enemy. To kill less than three birds with one stone did not suit our sanguinary purpose. We disliked the widow not so much for her sentimentality as for being the mother of Bill Conway; we disliked Mr. Meeks, not because he was insipid, like his own syrups, but because the widow loved him; Bill Conway we hated for himself.

Late one dark Saturday night in September we carried our plan into effect. On the following morning, as the orderly citizens wended their way to church past the widow's abode, their sober faces relaxed at beholding over her front door the well-known gilt Mortar and Pestle which usually stood on the top of a pole on the opposite corner; while the passers on that side of the street were equally amused and scandalized at seeing a placard bearing the following announcement tacked to the druggist's window-shutters:

Wanted, a Sempstress!

The naughty cleverness of the joke (which I should be sorry to defend) was recognized at once. It spread like wildfire over the town, and, though the mortar and placard were speedily removed, our triumph was complete. The whole community was on the broad grin, and our participation in the affair seemingly unsuspected.

It was those wicked soldiers at the fort!

CHAPTER X

I FIGHT CONWAY

THERE was one person, however, who cherished a strong suspicion that the Centipedes had had a hand in the business; and that person was Conway. His red hair seemed to change to a livelier red, and his sallow cheeks to a deeper sallow, as we glanced at him stealthily over the tops of our slates the next day in school. He knew we were watching him, and made sundry mouths and scowled in the most threatening way over his sums.

Conway had an accomplishment peculiarly his own — that of throwing his thumbs out of joint at will. Sometimes while absorbed in study, or on becoming nervous at recitation, he performed the feat unconsciously. Throughout this entire morning his thumbs were observed to be in a chronic state of dislocation, indicating great mental agitation on the part of the owner. We fully expected an outbreak from him at recess; but the intermission passed off tranquilly, somewhat to our disappointment.

At the close of the afternoon session it happened that Binny Wallace and myself, having got swamped in our Latin exercise, were detained in school for the purpose of refreshing our memories with a page of Mr. Andrews's perplexing irregular verbs. Binny Wallace finishing his task first, was dismissed. I followed shortly after, and, on stepping into the playground, saw my little friend plastered, as it were, up against the fence, and Conway standing in front of him ready to deliver a blow on the upturned, unprotected face, whose gentleness would have stayed any arm but a coward's.

Seth Rodgers, with both hands in his pockets, was leaning against the pump lazily enjoying the sport; but on seeing me sweep across the yard, whirling my strap of books in the air like a sling, he called out lustily, " Lay low, Conway! here 's young Bailey!"

Conway turned just in time to catch on his shoulder the blow intended for his head. He reached forward one of his long arms — he had arms like a windmill, that boy — and, grasping me by the hair, tore out quite a respectable handful. The tears flew to my eyes, but they were not the tears of defeat; they were merely the involuntary tribute which nature paid to the departed tresses.

In a second my little jacket lay on the ground, and I stood on guard, resting lightly on my right leg, and keeping my eye fixed steadily on Conway's — in all of which I was faithfully following the instructions of Phil Adams, whose father subscribed to a sporting journal.

Conway also threw himself into a defensive attitude, and there we were, glaring at each other, motionless, neither of us disposed to risk an attack, but both on the alert to resist one.   There is no telling how long we might have remained in that absurd position had we not been interrupted.

It was a custom with the larger pupils to return to the playground after school, and play base-ball until sundown.   The town authorities had prohibited ball-playing on the Square, and, there being no other available place, the boys fell back perforce on the school-yard.   Just at this crisis a dozen or so of the Templars entered the gate, and, seeing at a glance the belligerent status of Conway and myself, dropped bat and ball and rushed to the spot where we stood.

" Is it a fight ? " asked Phil Adams, who saw by our freshness that we had not yet got to work.

" Yes, it 's a fight," I answered, " unless Conway will ask Wallace's pardon, promise never to hector me in future — and put back my hair ! "

This last condition was rather a staggerer.

" I shan't do nothing of the sort," said Conway sulkily.

" Then the thing must go on," said Adams, with dignity.   " Rodgers, as I understand it, is your second, Conway ?   Bailey, come here. What 's the row about ? "

" He was thrashing Binny Wallace."

" No, I was n't," interrupted Conway ; " but I

was going to, because he knows who put Meeks's mortar over our door. And I know well enough who did it ; it was that sneaking little mulatter!" — pointing at me.

"Oh, by George!" I cried, reddening at the insult.

"Cool is the word," said Adams, as he bound a handkerchief round my head and carefully tucked away the long straggling locks that offered a

Preparing for the Battle

tempting advantage to the enemy. "Who ever heard of a fellow with such a head of hair going into action!" muttered Phil, twitching the handkerchief to ascertain if it were securely tied. He then loosened my gallowses (braces), and buckled them tightly above my hips. "Now, then, bantam, never say die!"

Conway regarded these business-like prepara-

tions with evident misgiving, for he called Rodgers to his side, and had himself arrayed in a
similar manner, though his hair was cropped so
close that you could not have taken hold of it with
a pair of tweezers.

"Is your man ready?" asked Phil Adams, addressing Rodgers.

"Ready!"

"Keep your back to the gate, Tom," whispered
Phil in my ear, "and you'll have the sun in his
eyes."

Behold us once more face to face, like David
and the Philistine.   Look at us as long as you
may; for this is all you shall see of the combat.
According to my thinking, the hospital teaches a
better lesson than the battlefield.   I will tell you
about my black eye, and my swollen lip, if you
will; but not a word of the fight.

You will get no description of it from me, simply because I think it would prove very poor reading, and not because I consider my revolt against
Conway's tyranny unjustifiable.

I had borne Conway's persecutions for many
months with lamb-like patience.   I might have
shielded myself by appealing to Mr. Grimshaw;
but no boy in the Temple Grammar School could
do that without losing caste.   Whether this was
just or not does not matter a pin, since it was so —
a traditionary law of the place.   The personal in-
convenience I suffered from my tormentor was

nothing to the pain he inflicted on me indirectly by his persistent cruelty to little Binny Wallace. I should have lacked the spirit of a hen if I had not resented it finally. I am glad that I faced Conway, and asked no favors, and got rid of him forever. I am glad that Phil Adams taught me to box, and I say to all youngsters : Learn to box, to ride, to pull an oar, and to swim. The occasion may come round when a decent proficiency in one or the rest of these accomplishments will be of service to you.

In one of the best books [1] ever written for boys are these words : —

"Learn to box, then, as you learn to play cricket and foot-ball. Not one of you will be the worse, but very much the better, for learning to box well. Should you never have to use it in earnest, there's no exercise in the world so good for the temper, and for the muscles of the back and legs.

"As for fighting, keep out of it, if you can, by all means. When the time comes, if ever it should, that you have to say 'Yes' or 'No' to a challenge to fight, say 'No' if you can — only take care you make it plain to yourself why you say 'No.' It's a proof of the highest courage, if done from true Christian motives. It's quite right and justifiable if done from a simple aversion to physical pain and danger. But don't say 'No' because you fear a licking and say or think it's because you fear

[1] *Tom Brown's School Days at Rugby.*

God, for that's neither Christian nor honest.   And if you do fight, fight it out; and don't give in while you can stand and see."

And don't give in while you can't ! say I.   For I could stand very little, and see not at all (having pummeled the school-pump for the last twenty seconds), when Conway retired from the field.   As Phil Adams stepped up to shake hands with me, he received a telling blow in the stomach; for all the fight was not out of me yet, and I mistook him for a new adversary.

Convinced of my error, I accepted his congratulations, with those of the other boys, blandly and blindly.   I remember that Binny Wallace wanted to give me his silver pencil - case.   The gentle soul had stood throughout the contest with his face turned to the fence, suffering untold agony.

Phil Adams shaking Hands

A good wash at the pump, and a cold key applied to my eye, refreshed me amazingly.

Escorted by two or three of the schoolfellows, I walked home through the pleasant autumn twilight, battered but triumphant.   As I went along, my cap cocked on one side to keep the chilly air from my eye, I felt that I was not only following my nose, but following it so closely, that I was in some danger of treading on it. I seemed to have nose enough for the whole party. My left cheek, also, was puffed out like a dumpling. I could not help saying to myself, " If *this* is victory, how about that other fellow ? "

Afterwards

" Tom," said Harry Blake, hesitating.

" Well ? "

" Did you see Mr. Grimshaw looking out of the recitation-room window just as we left the yard ? "

" No ; was he, though ? "

" I am sure of it."

" Then he must have seen all the row."

" Should n't wonder."

" No, he did n't," broke in Adams, "or he would have stopped it short metre ; but I guess he saw you pitching into the pump — which you did uncommonly strong — and of course he smelt mischief directly. "

" Well, it can't be helped now," I reflected.

" — As the monkey said when he fell out of the cocoanut tree," added Charley Marden, trying to make me laugh.

It was early candle-light when we reached the house. Miss Abigail, opening the front door,

started back at my hilarious appearance. I tried
to smile upon her sweetly, but the smile rippling
over my swollen cheek, and dying away like a
spent wave on my nose, produced an expression of
which Miss Abigail declared she had never seen
the like excepting on the face of a Chinese idol.

She hustled me unceremoniously into the presence of my grandfather in the sitting-room. Captain Nutter, as the recognized professional warrior
of our family, could not consistently take me to
task for fighting Conway ; nor was he disposed to
do so ; for the Captain was well aware of the long-
continued provocation I had endured.

"Ah, you rascal !" cried the old gentleman, after hearing my story, "just like me when I was
young — always in one kind of trouble or another.
I believe it runs in the family."

"I think," said Miss Abigail, without the faintest expression on her countenance, "that a tablespoonful of hot-dro— "

The Captain interrupted Miss Abigail peremp-
torily, directing her to make a shade out of card-
board and black silk, to tie over my eye. Miss
Abigail must have been possessed with the idea
that I had taken up pugilism as a profession, for
she turned out no fewer than six of these blinders.

"They'll be handy to have in the house," said
Miss Abigail grimly.

Of course, so great a breach of discipline was
not to be passed over by Mr. Grimshaw. He had,

as we suspected, witnessed the closing scene of the fight from the schoolroom window, and the next morning, after prayers, I was not wholly unprepared when Master Conway and myself were called up to the desk for examination. Conway, with a piece of court-plaster in the shape of a Maltese cross on his right cheek, and I with the silk patch over my left eye, caused a general titter through the room.

"Silence!" said Mr. Grimshaw sharply.

As the reader is already familiar with the leading points in the case of Bailey *versus* Conway, I shall not report the trial further than to say that Adams, Marden, and several other pupils testified to the fact that Conway had imposed on me ever since my first day at the Temple School. Their evidence also went to show that Conway was a quarrelsome character generally. Bad for Conway. Seth Rodgers, on the part of his friend, proved that I had struck the first blow. That was bad for me.

" If you please, sir," said Binny Wallace, holding up his hand for permission to speak, " Bailey did n't fight on his own account; he fought on my account, and, if you please, sir, I am the boy to be blamed, for I was the cause of the trouble."

This drew out the story of Conway's harsh treatment of the smaller boys. As Binny related the wrongs of his playfellows, saying very little of his own grievances, I noticed that Mr. Grimshaw's hand, unknown to himself perhaps, rested lightly from time to time on Wallace's sunny hair. The examination finished, Mr. Grimshaw leaned on the desk thoughtfully for a moment, and then said : —

"Every boy in this school knows that it is against the rules to fight. If one boy maltreats another, within school-bounds, or within school-hours, that is a matter for me to settle. The case should be laid before me. I disapprove of tale-bearing, I never encourage it in the slightest de-gree ; but when one pupil systematically persecutes a schoolmate, it is the duty of some head-boy to inform me. No pupil has a right to take the law into his own hands. If there is any fighting to be done, I am the person to be consulted. I disap-prove of boys' fighting ; it is unnecessary and un-christian. In the present instance, I consider every large boy in this school at fault; but as the offense is one of omission rather than commission, my punishment must rest only on the two boys convicted of misdemeanor. Conway loses his re-cess for a month, and Bailey has a page added to his Latin lessons for the next four recitations. I now request Bailey and Conway to shake hands in the presence of the school, and acknowledge their regret at what has occurred."

Conway and I approached each other slowly and cautiously, as if we were bent upon another hostile collision. We clasped hands in the tamest man-ner imaginable, and Conway mumbled, "I'm sorry I fought with you."

"I think you are," I replied, drily, "and I'm sorry I had to thrash you."

"You can go to your seats," said Mr. Grimshaw, turning his face aside to hide a smile. I am sure my apology was a very good one.

I never had any more trouble with Conway. He and his shadow, Seth Rodgers, gave me a wide berth for many months. Nor was Binny Wallace subjected to further molestation. Miss Abigail's sanitary stores, including a bottle of opodeldoc, were never called into requisition. The six black silk patches, with their elastic strings, are still dangling from a beam in the garret of the Nutter House, waiting for me to get into fresh difficulties.

CHAPTER XI

ALL ABOUT GYPSY

THIS record of my life at Rivermouth would be strangely incomplete did I not devote an entire chapter to Gypsy. I had other pets, of course ; for what healthy boy could long exist without numerous friends in the animal kingdom ? I had two white mice that were forever gnawing their way out of a pasteboard château, and crawling over my face when I lay asleep. I used to keep the pink-eyed little beggars in my bedroom, greatly to the annoyance of Miss Abigail, who was constantly fancying that one of the mice had secreted itself somewhere about her person.

I also owned a dog, a terrier, who managed in some inscrutable way to pick a quarrel with the moon, and on bright nights kept up such a ki-yi-ing in our back garden that we were finally forced to dispose of him at private sale. He was purchased by Mr. Oxford, the butcher. I protested against the arrangement, and ever afterwards, when we had sausages from Mr. Oxford's shop, I made believe I detected in them certain evidences that Cato had been foully dealt with.

Of birds I had no end — robins, purple-martins,

wrens, bulfinches, bobolinks, ringdoves, and pigeons. At one time I took solid comfort in the iniquitous society of a dissipated old parrot, who talked so terribly that the Rev. Wibird Hawkins,

happening to get a sample of Poll's vituperative powers, pronounced him " a benighted heathen," and advised the Captain to get rid of him. A brace of turtles supplanted the parrot in my affections ; the turtles gave way to rabbits ; and the rabbits in turn yielded to the superior charms of a small monkey, which the Captain bought of a sailor lately from the coast of Africa.

Rev. Wibird Hawkins and Poll

But Gypsy was the prime favorite, in spite of many rivals. I never grew weary of her. She was the most knowing little thing in the world. Her proper sphere in life — and the one to which she ultimately attained — was the saw-dust arena of a traveling circus. There was nothing short of the three R's, reading, 'riting, and 'rithmetic, that Gypsy could not be taught. The gift of speech was not hers, but the faculty of thought was.

My little friend, to be sure, was not exempt from certain graceful weaknesses, inseparable, perhaps, from the female character. She was very pretty, and she knew it. She was also passionately fond of dress — by which I mean her best harness. When she had this on, her curvetings and prancings were laughable, though in ordinary tackle she went along demurely enough. There was something in the enameled leather and the silver-washed mountings that chimed with her artistic sense. To have her mane braided, and a rose or a pansy stuck into her forelock, was to make her too conceited for anything.

She had another trait not rare among her sex. She liked the attentions of young gentlemen, while the society of girls bored her. She would drag them, sulkily, in the cart ; but as for permitting one of them in the saddle, the idea was preposterous. Once when Pepper Whitcomb's sister, in spite of our remonstrances, ventured to mount her, Gypsy gave a little indignant neigh, and tossed the gentle Emma heels over head in no time. But with any of the boys the mare was as docile as a lamb.

Her treatment of the several members of the family was comical. For the Captain she entertained a wholesome respect, and was always on her good behavior when he was around. As to Miss Abigail, Gypsy simply laughed at *her* — literally laughed, contracting her upper lip and displaying

all her snow-white teeth, as if something about Miss
Abigail struck her, Gypsy, as being extremely
ridiculous.

Kitty Collins, for some reason or another, was
afraid of the pony, or pretended to be. The saga-
cious little animal knew it, of course, and frequently, when Kitty was hanging out clothes near
the stable, the mare, being loose in the yard, would
make short plunges at her. Once Gypsy seized
the basket of
clothespins with
her teeth, and
rising on her
hind legs, pawing
the air with her
forefeet, followed
Kitty clear up
to the scullery
steps.

That part of
the yard was shut
off from the rest
by a gate ; but
no gate was proof
against Gypsy's
ingenuity. She
could let down

Gypsy's Lunch

bars, lift up latches, draw bolts, and turn all sorts
of buttons. This accomplishment rendered it
hazardous for Miss Abigail or Kitty to leave any

eatables on the kitchen table near the window. On one occasion Gypsy put in her head and lapped up six custard pies that had been placed by the casement to cool.

An account of my young lady's various pranks would fill a thick volume. A favorite trick of hers, on being requested to "walk like Miss Abigail," was to assume a little skittish gait so true to nature that Miss Abigail herself was obliged to admit the cleverness of the imitation.

The idea of putting Gypsy through a systematic course of instruction was suggested to me by a visit to the circus which gave an annual performance in Rivermouth. This show embraced among its attractions a number of trained Shetland ponies, and I determined that Gypsy should likewise have the benefit of a liberal education. I succeeded in teaching her to waltz, to fire a pistol by tugging at a string tied to the trigger, to lie down dead, to wink one eye, and to execute many other feats of a difficult nature. She took to her studies admirably, and enjoyed the whole thing as much as any one.

The monkey was a perpetual marvel to Gypsy. They became bosom-friends in an incredibly brief period, and were never easy out of each other's sight. Prince Zany — that 's what Pepper Whitcomb and I christened him one day, much to the disgust of the monkey, who bit a piece out of Pepper's nose — resided in the stable, and went to roost every night on the pony's back, where I usually found him in the morning. Whenever I rode out I was obliged to secure his Highness the Prince with a stout cord to the fence, he chattering all the time like a madman.

One afternoon as I was cantering through the crowded part of the town, I noticed that the people in the street stopped, stared at me, and fell to laughing. I turned round in the saddle, and there was Zany, with a great burdock leaf in his paw, perched up behind me on the crupper, as solemn as a judge.

After a few months, poor Zany sickened mysteriously and died. The dark thought occurred to me then, and comes back to me now with redoubled force, that Miss Abigail must have given him some hot-drops. Zany left a large circle of sorrowing friends, if not relatives. Gypsy, I think, never entirely recovered from the shock occasioned by his early demise. She became fonder of me, though; and one of her cunningest demonstrations was to escape from the stable-yard, and trot up to the door of the Temple Grammar School, where I would discover her at recess patiently waiting for me, with her forefeet on the second step, and wisps of straw standing out all over her, like quills upon the fretful porcupine.

I should fail if I tried to tell you how dear the pony was to me. Even hard, unloving men become attached to the horses they take care of ; so I, who was neither unloving nor hard, grew to love every glossy hair of the pretty little creature that depended on me for her soft straw bed and her daily modicum of oats. In my prayer at night I never forgot to mention Gypsy with the rest of the family — generally setting forth her claims first.

Whatever relates to Gypsy belongs properly to this narrative ; therefore I offer no apology for rescuing from oblivion, and boldly printing here a short composition which I wrote in the early part of my first quarter at the Temple Grammar School. It is my maiden effort in a difficult art, and is, perhaps, lacking in those graces of thought and style which are reached only after the severest practice.

Every Wednesday morning on entering school, each pupil was expected to lay his exercise on Mr. Grimshaw's desk ; the subject was usually selected

Prize No. 2

by Mr. Grimshaw himself, the Monday previous. With a humor characteristic of him, our teacher had instituted two prizes, one for the best and the other for the worst composition of the month. The first prize consisted of a penknife, or a pencil-case, or some such article dear to the heart of youth ; the second prize entitled the winner to wear for an hour or two a sort of conical paper cap, on the front of which was written, in tall letters, this modest admission : I AM A DUNCE!

The competitor who took prize No. 2 was not generally an object of envy.

My pulse beat high with pride and expectation that Wednesday morning, as I laid my essay, neatly folded, on the master's table. I firmly decline to say which prize I won; but here is the composition to speak for itself: —

The Horse

the horse is a Usefll animal He is nice to have. i have one. her name is gipsey. She bites, her main is very long. one Day i was washing her front Foot when she bent down her head and lifted me up by the trowsez and tumbled me into the water Pale that was standing near by, i hit her six times with a peace of hoop—the way of the transgressen is hard

T. Bailey

It is no small-author vanity that induces me to publish this stray leaf of natural history. I lay it before our young folks, not for their admiration, but for their criticism. Let each reader take his lead pencil and remorselessly correct the orthography, the capitalization, and the punctuation of the essay. I shall not feel hurt at seeing my treatise cut all to pieces; though I think highly of the production, not on account of its literary excellence, which I candidly admit is not overpowering, but because it was written years and years ago about Gypsy, by a little fellow who, when I strive to recall him, appears to me like a reduced ghost of my present self.

I am confident that any reader who has ever had pets, birds or animals, will forgive me for this brief digression.

CHAPTER XII

WINTER AT RIVERMOUTH

"I GUESS we 're going to have a regular old-fashioned snowstorm," said Captain Nutter, one bleak December morning, casting a peculiarly nautical glance skyward.

The Captain was always hazarding prophecies about the weather, which somehow never turned out according to his prediction. The vanes on the church steeples seemed to take a cynical pleasure in humiliating the dear old gentleman. If he said it was going to be a clear day, a dense sea fog was pretty certain to set in before noon. Once he caused a protracted drought by assuring us every morning, for six consecutive weeks, that it would rain in a few hours. But, sure enough, that afternoon it began snowing.

Now I had not seen a snowstorm since I was eighteen months old, and of course remembered nothing about it. A boy familiar from his infancy with the rigors of our New England winters can form no idea of the impression made on me by this natural phenomenon. My delight and surprise were as boundless as if the heavy gray sky had let down a shower of pond-lilies and white roses, instead of snowflakes. It happened to be a half-holiday, so I had nothing to do but watch the feathery crystals whirling hither and thither through the air. I stood by the sitting-room window gazing at the wonder until twilight shut out the novel scene.

We had had several slight flurries of hail and snow before, but this was a regular nor'easter.

Several inches of snow had already fallen. The rosebushes at the door drooped with the weight of their magical blossoms, and the two posts that held the garden gate were transformed into stately Turks, with white turbans, guarding the entrance to the Nutter House.

The storm increased at sundown, and continued with unabated violence through the night. The next morning, when I jumped out of bed, the sun was shining brightly, the cloudless heavens wore the tender azure of June, and the whole earth lay muffled up to the eyes, as it were, in a thick mantle of milk-white down.

It was a very deep snow. The Oldest Inhabitant (what would become of a New England town or village without its oldest inhabitant?) overhauled his almanacs, and pronounced it the deepest snow we had had for twenty years. It could n't have been much deeper without smothering us all. Our street was a sight to be seen, or, rather, it was a sight not to be seen; for very little street was visible. One huge drift completely banked up our front door and half covered my bedroom window.

There was no school that day, for all the thoroughfares were impassable. By twelve o'clock, however, the great snow-ploughs, each drawn by four yokes of oxen, broke a wagon-path through the principal streets; but the foot-passengers had a hard time of it floundering in the arctic drifts.

The Captain and I cut a tunnel, three feet wide and six feet high, from our front door to the sidewalk opposite. It was a beautiful cavern, with its walls and roof inlaid with mother-of-pearl and dia-

Talking over the Great Storm

monds. I am sure the ice palace of the Russian Empress, in Cowper's poem, was not a more superb piece of architecture.

The thermometer began falling shortly before sunset, and we had the bitterest cold night I ever experienced. This brought out the Oldest Inhabitant again the next day — and what a gay old boy he was for deciding everything! Our tunnel was turned into solid ice. A crust thick enough to bear men and horses had formed over the snow everywhere, and the air was alive with merry sleigh-bells. Icy stalactites, a yard long, hung from the eaves of the house, and the Turkish sentinels at the gate looked as if they had given up all hopes of ever being relieved from duty.

So the winter set in cold and glittering. Every-thing out of doors was sheathed in silver mail. To quote from Charley Marden, it was "cold enough to freeze the tail off a brass monkey" — an ob-servation which seemed to me extremely happy, though I knew little or nothing concerning the endurance of brass monkeys, having never seen one.

I had looked forward to the advent of the season with grave apprehensions, nerving myself to meet dreary nights and monotonous days; but summer itself was not more jolly than winter at Rivermouth. Snow-balling at school, skating on the Mill Pond, coasting by moonlight, long rides behind Gypsy in a brand-new little sleigh built expressly for her, were sports no less exhilarating than those which belonged to the sunny months. And then Thanks-giving! The nose of Memory — why should not Memory have a nose? — dilates with pleasure over the rich perfume of Miss Abigail's forty mince-pies, each one more delightful than the other, like the Sultan's forty wives. Christmas was another

red-letter day, though it was not so generally observed in New England as it is now.

The great wood-fire in the tiled chimney-place
made our sitting-room very cheerful of winter
nights. When the north-wind howled about the
eaves, and the sharp fingers of the sleet tapped
against the window-panes, it was nice to be so
warmly sheltered from
the storm. A dish of
apples and a pitcher
of chilly cider were
always served during
the evening. The
Captain had a funny
way of leaning back
in the chair and eat-
ing his apple with his
eyes closed. Some-
times I played domi-
noes with him, and

Eating his Apple

sometimes Miss Abigail read aloud to us, pronoun-
cing "to" *toe*, and sounding all the *eds*.

In a former chapter I alluded to Miss Abigail's
managing propensities. She had effected many
changes in the Nutter House before I came there
to live; but there was one thing against which
she had long contended without being able to overcome. This was the Captain's pipe. On first
taking command of the household, she prohibited
smoking in the sitting-room, where it had been the

old gentleman's custom to take a whiff or two of
the fragrant weed after meals. The edict went
forth — and so did the pipe. An excellent move,
no doubt; but then the house was his, and if he
saw fit to keep a tub of tobacco burning in the
middle of the parlor floor, he had a perfect right
to do so. However, he humored her in this as in
other matters, and smoked by stealth, like a guilty
creature, in the barn, or about the gardens. That
was practicable in summer, but in winter the Captain was hard put to it. When he could not stand
it longer, he retreated to his bedroom and barri-
caded the door. Such was the position of affairs
at the time of which I write.

One morning, a few days after the great snow,
as Miss Abigail was dusting the chronometer in
the hall, she beheld Captain Nutter slowly descend-
ing the staircase, with a long clay pipe in his
mouth. Miss Abigail could hardly credit her own
eyes.

"Dan'el!" she gasped, retiring heavily on the
hat-rack.

The tone of reproach with which this word was
uttered failed to produce the slightest effect on
the Captain, who merely removed the pipe from
his lips for an instant, and blew a cloud into the
chilly air. The thermometer stood at two degrees
below zero in our hall.

"Dan'el!" cried Miss Abigail, hysterically —
"Dan'el, don't come near me!" Whereupon she

fainted away ; for the smell of tobacco smoke always made her deadly sick.

Kitty Collins rushed from the kitchen with a
basin of water, and set to work bathing Miss Abigail's temples and chaffing her hands.   I thought
my grandfather rather cruel, as he stood there

Kitty and Tom enjoying the Joke

with a half-smile on his countenance, complacently
watching Miss Abigail's sufferings.   When she
was "brought to," the Captain sat down beside
her, and, with a lovely twinkle in his eye, said
softly :

"Abigail, my dear, *there was n't any tobacco in
that pipe!*   It was a new pipe.   I fetched it down
for Tom to blow soap-bubbles with."

At these words Kitty Collins hurried away, her features working strangely. Several minutes later I came upon her in the scullery with the greater portion of a crash towel stuffed into her mouth. "Miss Abygil smelt the terbacca with her oi!" cried Kitty, partially removing the cloth, and then immediately stopping herself up again.

The Captain's joke furnished us — that is, Kitty and me — with mirth for many a day ; as to Miss Abigail, I think she never wholly pardoned him. After this, Captain Nutter gradually gave up smoking, which is an untidy, injurious, disgraceful, and highly pleasant habit.

A boy's life in a secluded New England town in winter does not afford many points for illustration. Of course he gets his ears or toes frostbitten ; of course he smashes his sled against another boy's ; of course he bangs his head on the ice, and he 's a lad of no enterprise whatever if he does not manage to skate into an eel-hole, and be brought home half-drowned. All these things happened to me ; but, as they lack novelty, I pass them over to tell you about the famous snow-fort which we built on Slatter's Hill.

CHAPTER XIII

THE SNOW-FORT ON SLATTER'S HILL

THE memory of man, even that of the Oldest Inhabitant, runneth not back to the time when there did not exist a feud between the North End and the South End boys of Rivermouth.

The origin of the feud is involved in mystery; it is impossible to say which party was the first aggressor in the far-off ante-revolutionary ages; but the fact remains that the youngsters of those antipodal sections entertained a mortal hatred for each other, and that this hatred had been handed down from generation to generation, like Miles Standish's punch-bowl.

I know not what laws, natural or unnatural, regulated the warmth of the quarrel; but at some seasons it raged more violently than at others. This winter both parties were unusually lively and antagonistic. Great was the wrath of the South-Enders when they discovered that the North-Enders had thrown up a fort on the crown of Slatter's Hill.

Slatter's Hill, or No-man's-land, as it was generally called, was a rise of ground covering, perhaps, an acre and a quarter, situated on an imaginary line, marking the boundary between the two districts. An immense stratum of granite, which here and there thrust out a wrinkled bowlder, prevented the site from being used for building purposes. The street ran on either side of the hill, from one part of which a quantity of rock had been removed to form the underpinning of the new jail. This excavation made the approach from that point all but impossible, especially when the ragged ledges were a-glitter with ice. You see what a spot it was for a snow-fort.

One evening twenty or thirty of the North-Enders quietly took possession of Slatter's Hill, and threw up a strong line of breastworks, something after this shape :

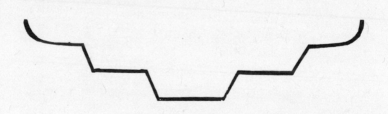

The rear of the intrenchment, being protected by the quarry, was left open. The walls were four feet high, and twenty-two inches thick, strengthened at the angles by stakes driven firmly into the ground.

Fancy the rage of the South-Enders the next day, when they spied our snowy citadel, with Jack

Harris's red silk pocket-handkerchief floating defiantly from the flagstaff.

In less than an hour it was known all over town, in military circles at least, that the " Puddle-dockers" and the " River-rats" (these were the derisive sub-titles bestowed on our South-End foes) intended to attack the fort that Saturday afternoon.

At two o'clock all the fighting boys of the Temple Grammar School, and as many recruits as we could muster, lay behind the walls of Fort Slatter, with three hundred compact snow-balls piled up in pyramids, awaiting the approach of the enemy. The enemy was not slow in making his approach — fifty strong, headed by one Mat Ames. Our forces were under the command of General J. Harris.

Before the action commenced, a meeting was arranged between the rival commanders, who drew up and signed certain rules and regulations respecting the conduct of the battle. As it was impossible for the North-Enders to occupy the fort permanently, it was stipulated that the South-Enders should assault it only on Wednesday and Saturday afternoons between the hours of two and six. For them to take possession of the place at any other time was not to constitute a capture, but, on the contrary, was to be considered a dishonorable and cowardly act.

The North-Enders, on the other hand, agreed to give up the fort whenever ten of the storming party succeeded in obtaining at one time a footing on the parapet, and were able to hold the same for the space of two minutes. Both sides were to abstain from putting pebbles into their snow-balls, nor was it permissible to use frozen ammunition.

A snow-ball soaked in water and left out to cool was a projectile which in previous years had been resorted to with disastrous results.

These preliminaries settled, the commanders retired to their respective

The Commanders

corps. The interview had taken place on the hillside between the opposing lines.

General Harris divided his men into two bodies ; the first comprised the most skillful marksmen, or gunners ; the second, the reserve force, was composed of the strongest boys, whose duty it was to repel the scaling parties, and to make occasional sallies for the purpose of capturing prisoners, who were bound by the articles of treaty to faithfully serve under our flag until they were exchanged at the close of the day.

The repellers were called light infantry; but when they carried on operations beyond the fort they became cavalry. It was also their duty, when not otherwise engaged, to manufacture snow-balls. The General's staff consisted of five Templars (I among the number, with the rank of Major), who carried the General's orders and looked after the wounded.

General Mat Ames, a veteran commander, was no less wide-awake in the disposition of his army. Five companies, each numbering but six men, in order not to present too big a target to our sharp-shooters, were to charge the fort from different points, their advance being covered by a heavy fire from the gunners posted in the rear. Each scaler was provided with only two rounds of ammunition, which were not to be used until he had mounted the breastwork and could deliver his shots on our heads.

The following diagram represents the interior of the fort just previous to the assault. Nothing on earth could represent the state of things after the first volley.

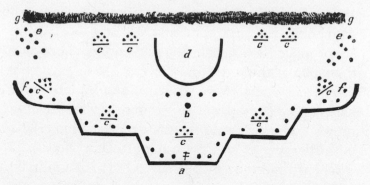

a. Flagstaff.   c. Ammunition.   f, f. Gunners in position.
b. General Harris and his Staff.   d. Hospital.   g, g. The quarry.
                                   e, e, Reserve corps.

The enemy was posted thus :

a, a. The five attacking columns.   b, b. Artillery.   c. General Ames's head-
                              quarters.

The thrilling moment had now arrived. If I
had been going into a real engagement I could not
have been more deeply impressed by the importance of the occasion.

The fort opened fire first — a single ball from
the dexterous hand of General Harris taking General Ames in the very pit of his stomach. A
cheer went up from Fort Slatter. In an instant
the air was thick with flying missiles, in the midst
of which we dimly descried the storming parties
sweeping up the hill, shoulder to shoulder. The

shouts of the leaders, and the snow-balls bursting like shells about our ears, made it very lively.

Not more than a dozen of the enemy succeeded in reaching the crest of the hill; five of these clambered upon the icy walls, where they were instantly grabbed by the legs and jerked into the fort.   The rest retired confused and blinded by our well-directed fire.

When General Harris (with his right eye bunged up) said, "Soldiers, I am proud of you!" my heart swelled in my bosom.

The victory, however, had not been without its price.   Six North-Enders, having rushed out to harass the discomfited enemy, were gallantly cut off by General Ames and captured.   Among these were Lieutenant P. Whitcomb (who had no business to join in the charge, being weak in the knees) and Captain Fred Langdon, of General Harris's staff.   Whitcomb was one of the most notable shots on our side, though he was not much to boast of in a rough-and-tumble fight, owing to the weakness before mentioned.   General Ames put him among the gunners, and we were quickly made aware of the loss we had sustained, by receiving a frequent artful ball which seemed to light with unerring instinct on any nose that was the least bit exposed.   I have known one of Pepper's snow-balls, fired point-blank, to turn a corner and hit a boy who considered himself absolutely safe.

But we had no time for vain regrets.   The battle raged. Already there were two bad cases of black-eye, and one of nose-bleed, in the hospital.

It was glorious excitement, those pell-mell onslaughts and hand-to-hand struggles. Twice we were within an ace of being driven from our stronghold, when General Harris and his staff leaped recklessly upon the ramparts and hurled the besiegers heels over head downhill.

At sunset the garrison of Fort Slatter was still unconquered, and the South - Enders, in a solid phalanx, marched off whistling " Yankee Doodle," while we cheered and jeered them until they were out of hearing.

General Ames remained behind to effect an exchange of prisoners. We held thirteen of his men, and he eleven of ours. General Ames proposed to call it an even thing, since many of his eleven prisoners were officers, while nearly all our thirteen captives were privates. A dispute arising on this point, the two noble generals came to fisticuffs, and in the fracas our brave commander got his remaining well eye badly damaged. This did not prevent him from writing a general order the next day, on a slate, in which he complimented the troops on their heroic behavior.

On the following Wednesday the siege was renewed. I forget whether it was on that afternoon or the next that we lost Fort Slatter; but lose it we did, with much valuable ammunition and several men. After a series of desperate assaults,

Holding the Fort on Slatter's Hill

we forced General Ames to capitulate ; and he, in turn, made the place too hot to hold us.   So from day to day the tide of battle surged to and fro, sometimes favoring our arms, and sometimes those of the enemy.

General Ames handled his men with great skill ; his deadliest foe could not deny that.   Once he out-generaled our commander in the following manner :   He massed his gunners on our left and opened a brisk fire, under cover of which a single company (six men) advanced on that angle of the fort.   Our reserves on the right rushed over to defend the threatened point.   Meanwhile, four companies of the enemy's scalers made a détour round the foot of the hill, and dashed into Fort Slatter without opposition.   At the same moment General Ames's gunners closed in on our left, and there we were between two fires.   Of course we had to vacate the fort.   A cloud rested on General Harris's military reputation until his superior tactics enabled him to dispossess the enemy.

As the winter wore on, the war-spirit waxed fiercer and fiercer.   Finally the provision against using heavy substances in the snow-balls was disregarded.   A ball stuck full of sand-bird shot came tearing into Fort Slatter.   In retaliation, General Harris ordered a broadside of shells ; i. e. snow-balls containing marbles.   After this, both sides never failed to freeze their ammunition.

It was no longer child's play to march up to the

walls of Fort Slatter, nor was the position of the besieged less perilous. At every assault three or four boys on each side were disabled. It was not an infrequent occurrence for the combatants to hold up a flag of truce while they removed some insensible comrade.

Matters grew worse and worse. Seven North-Enders had been seriously wounded, and a dozen South-Enders were reported on the sick list. The selectmen of the town awoke to the fact of what was going on, and detailed a posse of police to prevent further disturbance. The boys at the foot of the hill, South-Enders as it happened, finding themselves assailed in the rear and on the flank, turned round and attempted to beat off the watch-men. In this they were sustained by numerous volunteers from the fort, who looked upon the interference as tyrannical.

The watch were determined fellows, and charged the boys valiantly, driving them all into the fort, where we made common cause, fighting side by side like the best of friends. In vain the four guardians of the peace rushed up the hill, flourish-ing their clubs and calling upon us to surrender. They could not get within ten yards of the fort, our fire was so destructive. In one of the onsets a man named Mugridge, more valorous than his peers, threw himself upon the parapet, when he was seized by twenty pairs of hands, and dragged inside the breastwork, where fifteen boys sat down on him to keep him quiet.

Perceiving that it was impossible with their small number to dislodge us, the watch sent for reinforcements. Their call was responded to, not only by the whole constabulary force (eight men), but by a numerous body of citizens, who

The Unsuccessful Attack

had become alarmed at the prospect of a riot. This formidable array brought us to our senses : we began to think that maybe discretion was the better part of valor. General Harris and General Ames, with their respective staffs, held a council of war in the hospital, and a backward movement was decided on. So, after one grand farewell volley, we fled, sliding, jumping, rolling, tumbling down the quarry at the rear of the fort, and escaped without losing a man.

But we lost Fort Slatter forever. Those battle-scarred ramparts were razed to the ground, and humiliating ashes sprinkled over the historic spot, near which a solitary lynx-eyed policeman was seen prowling from time to time during the rest of the winter.

The event passed into a legend, and afterwards, when later instances of pluck and endurance were spoken of, the boys would say, " By golly! you ought to have been at the fights on Slatter's Hill!"

CHAPTER XIV

THE CRUISE OF THE DOLPHIN

IT was spring again. The snow had faded away like a dream, and we were awakened, so to speak, by the sudden chirping of robins in our back garden. Marvelous transformation of snow-drifts into lilacs, wondrous miracle of the unfolding leaf! We read in the Holy Book how our Saviour, at the marriage-feast, changed the water into wine; we pause and wonder, but every hour a greater miracle is wrought at our feet, if we have but eyes to see it.

I had now been a year at Rivermouth. If you do not know what sort of boy I was, it is not because I have been lacking in frankness with you. Of my progress at school I say little; for this is a story, pure and simple, and not a treatise on education. Behold me, however, well up in most of the classes. I have worn my Latin grammar into tatters, and am in the first book of Virgil. I interlard my conversation at home with easy quotations from that poet, and impress Captain Nutter with a lofty notion of my learning. I am likewise translating Les Aventures de Télémaque from the French, and shall tackle Blair's Lectures the next term. I am ashamed of my crude composition about The Horse, and can do better now. Sometimes my head almost aches with the variety of my knowledge. I consider Mr. Grimshaw the greatest scholar that ever lived, and I do not know which I would rather be — a learned man like him, or a circus-rider.

My thoughts revert to this particular spring more frequently than to any other period of my boyhood, for it was marked by an event that left an indelible impression on my memory. As I pen these pages, I feel that I am writing of something which happened yesterday, so vividly it all comes back to me.

Every Rivermouth boy looks upon the sea as being in some way mixed up with his destiny. While he is yet a baby lying in his cradle, he hears the dull, far-off boom of the breakers ; when he is older, he wanders by the sandy shore, watching the waves that come plunging up the beach like white-maned sea-horses, as Thoreau calls them ; his eye follows the lessening sail as it fades into the blue horizon, and he burns for the time when he shall stand on the quarter-deck of his own ship, and go sailing proudly across that mysterious waste of waters.

Then the town itself is full of hints and flavors of the sea. The gables and roofs of the houses facing eastward are covered with red rust, like the flukes of old anchors ; a salty smell pervades the

air, and dense gray fogs, the very breath of Ocean,
periodically creep up into the quiet streets and
envelop everything.   The terrific storms that
lash the coast ; the kelp and spars, and sometimes
the bodies of drowned men, tossed on shore by the
scornful waves ; the shipyards, the wharves, and
the tawny fleet of fishing-smacks yearly fitted out
at Rivermouth — these things, and a hundred
other, feed the imagination and fill the brain of
every healthy boy with dreams of adventure.   He
learns to swim almost as soon as he can walk ; he
draws in with his mother's milk the art of hand-
ling an oar : he is born a sailor, whatever he may
turn out to be afterwards.

To own the whole or a portion of a row-boat is
his earliest ambition.   No wonder that I, born to
this life, and coming back to it with freshest sym-
pathies, should have caught the prevailing in-
fection.   No wonder I longed to buy a part of the
trim little sail-boat Dolphin, which chanced just
then to be in the market.   This was in the latter
part of May.

Three shares, at five or six dollars each, I forget which, had already been taken by Phil Adams,
Fred Langdon, and Binny Wallace.   The fourth
and remaining share hung fire.   Unless a pur-
chaser could be found for this, the bargain was
to fall through.

I am afraid I required but slight urging to join
in the investment.   I had four dollars and fifty

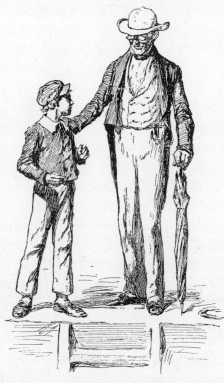

I faced Captain Nutter

cents on hand, and the treasurer of the Centipedes advanced me the balance, receiving my silver pencil-case as ample security. It was a proud moment when I stood on the wharf with my partners, inspecting the Dolphin, moored at the foot of a very slippery flight of steps. She was painted white with a green stripe outside, and on the stern a yellow dolphin, with its scarlet mouth wide open, stared with a surprised expression at its own reflection in the water. The boat was a great bargain.

I whirled my cap in the air, and ran to the stairs leading down from the wharf, when a hand was laid gently on my shoulder. I turned, and faced Captain Nutter. I never saw such an old sharp-eye as he was in those days.

I knew he would not be angry with me for buying a row-boat ; but I also knew that the little bowsprit suggesting a jib, and the tapering mast ready for its few square feet of canvas, were trifles not likely to meet his approval. As far as rowing on the river, among the wharves, was concerned, the Captain had long since withdrawn his decided objections, having convinced himself, by going out with me several times, that I could manage a pair of sculls as well as anybody.

I was right in my surmises. He commanded me, in the most emphatic terms, never to go out in the Dolphin without leaving the mast in the boat-house. This curtailed my anticipated sport, but the pleasure of having a pull whenever I wanted it remained. I never disobeyed the Captain's orders touching the sail, though I sometimes extended my row beyond the points he had indicated.

The river was dangerous for sail-boats. Squalls, without the slightest warning, were of frequent occurrence ; scarcely a year passed that three or four persons were not drowned under the very windows of the town, and these, oddly enough, were generally sea-captains, who either did not understand the river, or lacked the skill to handle a small craft.

A knowledge of such disasters, one of which I witnessed, consoled me somewhat when I saw Phil Adams skimming over the water in a spanking

breeze with every stitch of canvas set.   There
were few better yachtsmen than Phil Adams.   He
usually went sailing alone, for both Langdon and
Binny Wallace were under the same restrictions I
was.

Not long after the purchase of the boat, we
planned an excursion to Sandpeep Island, the
last of the islands in the harbor.   We purposed to
start early in the morning, and return with the
tide in the moonlight.   Our only difficulty was
to obtain a whole day's exemption from school,
the customary half-holiday not being long enough
for our picnic.   Somehow, we could not work it;
but fortune arranged it for us.   I may say here,
that, whatever else I did, I never played truant
("hookey" we called it) in my life.

One afternoon the four owners of the Dolphin
exchanged significant glances when Mr. Grimshaw
announced from the desk that there would be no
school the following day, he having just received
intelligence of the death of his uncle in Boston.
I was sincerely attached to Mr. Grimshaw, but I
am afraid that the death of his uncle did not affect
me as it ought to have done.

We were up before sunrise the next morning,
in order to take advantage of the flood tide, which
waits for no man.   Our preparations for the cruise
were made the previous evening.   In the way of
eatables and drinkables, we had stored in the
stern of the Dolphin a generous bag of hard-tack

(for the chowder), a piece of pork to fry the cunners in, three gigantic apple-pies (bought at Pettingil's), half a dozen lemons, and a keg of spring
water — the last-named article we slung over the
side, to keep it cool, as soon as we got under way.
The crockery and the bricks for our camp-stove
we placed in the bows with the groceries, which
included sugar, pepper, salt, and a bottle of pickles.
Phil Adams contributed to the outfit a small tent
of unbleached cotton cloth, under which we intended to take our nooning.

We unshipped the mast, threw in an extra oar,
and were ready to embark. I do not believe that
Christopher Columbus, when he started on his
rather successful voyage of discovery, felt half the
responsibility and importance that weighed upon
me as I sat on the middle seat of the Dolphin,
with my oar resting in the row-lock. I wonder if
Christopher Columbus quietly slipped out of the
house without letting his estimable family know
what he was up to? Charley Marden, whose
father had promised to cane him if he ever stepped
foot on sail or row boat, came down to the wharf
in a sour-grape humor, to see us off. Nothing
would tempt *him* to go out on the river in such a
crazy clam-shell of a boat. He pretended that he
did not expect to behold us alive again, and tried
to throw a wet blanket over the expedition.

"Guess you'll have a squally time of it," said
Charley, casting off the painter. "I'll drop in at

old Newbury's" (Newbury was the parish under-
taker) "and leave word, as I go along!"

"Bosh!" muttered Phil Adams, sticking the
boat-hook into the string-piece of the wharf, and
sending the Dolphin half a dozen yards towards
the current.

How calm and lovely the river was! Not a
ripple stirred on the glassy surface, broken only
by the sharp cutwater of our tiny craft. The sun,
as round and red as an August moon, was by this
time peering above the water-line.

The town had drifted behind us, and we were
entering among the group of islands. Sometimes
we could almost touch with our boat-hook the
shelving banks on either side. As we neared the
mouth of the harbor, a little breeze now and then
wrinkled the blue water, shook the spangles from
the foliage, and gently lifted the spiral mist-
wreaths that still clung along shore. The meas-
ured dip of our oars and the drowsy twitterings of
the birds seemed to mingle with, rather than break,
the enchanted silence that reigned about us.

The scent of the new clover comes back to me
now, as I recall that delicious morning when we
floated away in a fairy boat down a river like a
dream!

The sun was well up when the nose of the Dolphin nestled against the snow-white bosom of
Sandpeep Island. This island, as I have said
before, was the last of the cluster, one side of it

On Sandpeep Island

being washed by the sea. We landed on the river side, the sloping sands and quiet water affording us a good place to moor the boat.

It took us an hour or more to transport our stores to the spot selected for the encampment. Having pitched our tent, using the five oars to support the canvas, we got out our lines, and went down the rocks seaward to fish. It was early for cunners, but we were lucky enough to catch as nice a mess as ever you saw. A cod for the chowder was not so easily secured. At last Binny Wallace hauled in a plump little fellow crusted all over with flaky silver.

To skin the fish, build our fireplace, and cook the chowder, kept us busy the next two hours.

The fresh air and the exercise had given us the appetites of wolves, and we were about famished by the time the savory mixture was ready for our clam-shell saucers.

I shall not insult the rising generation on the seaboard by telling them how delectable is a chowder compounded and eaten in this Robinson Crusoe fashion. As for the boys who live inland, and know naught of such marine feasts, my heart is full of pity for them. What wasted lives! Not to know the delights of a clam-bake, not to love chowder, to be ignorant of lob-scouse!

How happy we were, we four, sitting cross-legged in the crisp salt grass, with the invigorating sea-breeze blowing gratefully through our hair! What a joyous thing was life, and how far off seemed death — death, that lurks in all pleasant places, and was so near!

The banquet finished, Phil Adams drew from his pocket a handful of sweet-fern cigars; but as none of the party could indulge without imminent risk of becoming ill, we all, on one pretext or another, declined, and Phil smoked by himself.

The wind had freshened by this, and we found it comfortable to put on the jackets which had been thrown aside in the heat of the day. We strolled along the beach and gathered large quantities of the fairy-woven Iceland moss, which, at certain seasons, is washed to these shores; then we played at ducks and drakes, and then, the sun being sufficiently low, we went in bathing.

Before our bath was ended a slight change had come over the sky and sea; fleecy-white clouds scudded here and there, and a muffled moan from the breakers caught our ears from time to time. While we were dressing, a few hurried drops of rain came lisping down, and we adjourned to the tent to wait the passing of the squall.

"We're all right, anyhow," said Phil Adams. "It won't be much of a blow, and we'll be as snug as a bug in a rug, here in the tent, particularly if we have that lemonade which some of you fellows were going to make."

By an oversight, the lemons had been left in the boat. Binny Wallace volunteered to go for them.

"Put an extra stone on the painter, Binny," said Adams, calling after him; "it would be awkward to have the Dolphin give us the slip and return to port minus her passengers."

"That it would," answered Binny, scrambling down the rocks.

Sandpeep Island is diamond shaped — one point running out into the sea, and the other looking towards the town. Our tent was on the river side. Though the Dolphin was also on the same side, it lay out of sight by the beach at the farther extremity of the island.

Binny Wallace had been absent five or six minutes, when we heard him calling our several names in tones that indicated distress or surprise, we could not tell which. Our first thought was, "The boat has broken adrift!"

We sprung to our feet and hastened down to the beach. On turning the bluff which hid the mooring-place from our view, we found the conjecture correct. Not only was the Dolphin afloat, but poor little Binny Wallace was standing in the bows with his arms stretched helplessly towards us — *drifting out to sea!*

"Head the boat in shore!" shouted Phil Adams.

Wallace ran to the tiller; but the slight cockleshell merely swung round and drifted broadside on. Oh, if we had but left a single scull in the Dolphin!

"Can you swim it?" cried Adams desperately,

using his hand as a speaking-trumpet, for the distance between the boat and the island widened momently.

Binny Wallace looked down at the sea, which was covered with white caps, and made a despairing gesture. He knew, and we knew, that the stoutest swimmer could not live forty seconds in those angry waters.

A wild, insane light came into Phil Adams's eyes, as he stood knee-deep in the boiling surf, and for an instant I think he meditated plunging into the ocean after the receding boat.

The sky darkened, and an ugly look stole rapidly over the broken surface of the sea.

Binny Wallace half rose from his seat in the stern, and waved his hand to us in token of farewell. In spite of the distance, increasing every instant, we could see his face plainly. The anxious expression it wore at first had passed. It was pale and meek now, and I love to think there was a kind of halo about it, like that which painters place around the forehead of a saint. So he drifted away.

The sky grew darker and darker. It was only by straining our eyes through the unnatural twilight that we could keep the Dolphin in sight. The figure of Binny Wallace was no longer visible, for the boat itself had dwindled to a mere white dot on the black water. Now we lost it, and our hearts stopped throbbing ; and now the speck appeared again, for an instant, on the crest of a high wave.

Finally, it went out like a spark, and we saw it no more. Then we gazed at each other, and dared not speak.

Absorbed in following the course of the boat, we had scarcely noticed the huddled inky clouds

Drifting Away

that sagged down all around us. From these threatening masses, seamed at intervals with pale lightning, there now burst a heavy peal of thunder that shook the ground under our feet. A sud-

den squall struck the sea, ploughing deep white
furrows into it, and at the same instant a single
piercing shriek rose above the tempest — the
frightened cry of a gull swooping over the island.
How it startled us!

It was impossible any longer to keep our footing on the beach.   The wind and the breakers
would have swept us into the ocean if we had not
clung to each other with the desperation of drown-
ing men.   Taking advantage of a momentary lull,
we crawled up the sands on our hands and knees,
and, pausing in the lee of the granite ledge to gain
breath, returned to the camp, where we found that
the gale had snapped all the fastenings of the tent
but one.   Held by this, the puffed-out canvas
swayed in the wind like a balloon.   It was a task
of some difficulty to secure it, which we did by
beating down the canvas with the oars.

After several trials, we succeeded in setting up
the tent on the leeward side of the ledge.   Blinded
by the vivid flashes of lightning, and drenched by
the rain, which fell in torrents, we crept, half dead
with fear and anguish, under our flimsy shelter.
Neither the anguish nor the fear was on our own
account, for we were comparatively safe, but for
poor little Binny Wallace, driven out to sea in the
merciless gale.   We shuddered to think of him in
that frail shell, drifting on and on to his grave,
the sky rent with lightning over his head, and the
green abysses yawning beneath him.   We fell to

crying, the three of us, and cried I know not how long.

Meanwhile the storm raged with augmented fury. We were obliged to hold on to the ropes of the tent to prevent it blowing away. The spray from the river leaped several yards up the rocks and clutched at us malignantly. The very island trembled with the concussions of the sea beating upon it, and at times I fancied that it had broken loose from its foundation, and was floating off with us. The breakers, streaked with angry phosphorus, were fearful to look at.

The wind rose higher and higher, cutting long slits in the tent, through which the rain poured incessantly. To complete the sum of our miseries, the night was at hand. It came down suddenly, at last, like a curtain, shutting in Sandpeep Island from all the world.

It was a dirty night, as the sailors say. The darkness was something that could be felt as well as seen — it pressed down upon one with a cold, clammy touch. Gazing into the hollow blackness, all sorts of imaginable shapes seemed to start forth from vacancy — brilliant colors, stars, prisms, and dancing lights. What boy, lying awake at night, has not amused or terrified himself by peopling the spaces around his bed with these phenomena of his own eyes?

"I say," whispered Fred Langdon, at length, clutching my hand, "don't you see things — out there — in the dark?"

"Yes, yes — Binny Wallace's face!"

I added to my own nervousness by making this avowal; though for the last ten minutes I had seen little besides that star-pale face with its angelic hair and brows. First a slim yellow circle, like the nimbus round the moon, took shape and grew sharp against the darkness; then this faded gradually, and there was the Face, wearing the same sad, sweet look it wore when he waved his hand to us across the awful water. This optical illusion kept repeating itself.

"And I too," said Adams. "I see it every now and then, outside there. What would n't I give if it really was poor little Wallace looking in at us! O boys, how shall we dare to go back to the town without him? I 've wished a hundred times, since we 've been sitting here, that I was in his place, alive or dead!"

We dreaded the approach of morning as much as we longed for it. The morning would tell us all. Was it possible for the Dolphin to outride such a storm? There was a lighthouse on Mackerel Reef, which lay directly in the course the boat had taken when it disappeared. If the Dolphin had caught on this reef, perhaps Binny Wallace was safe. Perhaps his cries had been heard by the keeper of the light. The man owned a life-boat, and had rescued several persons. Who could tell?

Such were the questions we asked ourselves again and again, as we lay in each other's arms waiting for daybreak. What an endless night it was! I have known months that did not seem so long.

Our position was irksome rather than perilous; for the day was certain to bring us relief from the town, where our prolonged absence, together with the storm, had no doubt excited the liveliest alarm for our safety. But the cold, the darkness, and the suspense were hard to bear.

Our soaked jackets had chilled us to the bone. To keep warm, we lay huddled together so closely that we could hear our hearts beat above the tumult of sea and sky.

After a while we grew very hungry, not having broken our fast since early in the day. The rain had turned the hard-tack into a sort of dough; but it was better than nothing.

We used to laugh at Fred Langdon for always carrying in his pocket a small vial of essence of peppermint or sassafras, a few drops of which, sprinkled on a lump of loaf-sugar, he seemed to consider a great luxury. I do not know what would have become of us at this crisis if it had not been for that omnipresent bottle of hot stuff. We poured the stinging liquid over our sugar, which had kept dry in a sardine-box, and warmed ourselves with frequent doses.

After four or five hours the rain ceased, the wind died away to a moan, and the sea — no longer raging like a maniac — sobbed and sobbed with a piteous human voice all along the coast. And well it might, after that night's work. Twelve sail of the Gloucester fishing fleet had gone down with every soul on board, just outside of Whale's-back Light. Think of the wide grief that follows in the wake of one wreck; then think of the despairing women who wrung their hands and wept, the next morning, in the streets of Gloucester, Marblehead, and Newcastle!

Though our strength was nearly spent, we were too cold to sleep. Once I sunk into a troubled doze, when I seemed to hear Charley Marden's parting words, only it was the Sea that said them. After that I threw off the drowsiness whenever it threatened to overcome me.

Fred Langdon was the earliest to discover a filmy, luminous streak in the sky, the first glimmering of sunrise.

" Look, it is nearly daybreak ! "

While we were following the direction of his finger, a sound of distant oars fell upon our ears.

We listened breathlessly, and as the dip of the blades became more audible, we discerned two foggy lights, like will-o'-the-wisps, floating on the river.

Running down to the water's edge, we hailed the boats with all our might. The call was heard, for the oars rested a moment in the row-locks, and then pulled in towards the island.

It was two boats from the town, in the foremost

of which we could now make out the figures of
Captain Nutter and Binny Wallace's father.   We
shrunk back on seeing *him.*

" Thank God!" cried Mr. Wallace fervently, as
he leaped from the wherry without waiting for the
bow to touch the beach.

But when he saw only three boys standing on
the sands, his eye wandered restlessly about in
quest of the fourth ; then a deadly pallor over-
spread his features.

Our story was soon told.   A solemn silence fell
upon the crowd of rough boatmen gathered round,
interrupted only by a stifled sob from one poor old
man, who stood apart trom the rest.

The sea was still running too high for any small
boat to venture out ; so it was arranged that the
wherry should take us back to town, leaving the
yawl, with a picked crew, to hug the island until
daybreak, and then set forth in search of the Dolphin.

Though it was barely sunrise when we reached
town, there were a great many persons assembled
at the landing eager for intelligence from missing
boats.   Two picnic parties had started down river
the day before, just previous to the gale, and nothing had been heard of them.   It turned out that
the pleasure-seekers saw their danger in time, and
ran ashore on one of the least exposed islands,
where they passed the night.   Shortly after our
own arrival they appeared off Rivermouth, much

to the joy of their friends, in two shattered, dismasted boats.

The excitement over, I was in a forlorn state, physically and mentally. Captain Nutter put me to bed between hot blankets, and sent Kitty Collins for the doctor. I was wandering in my mind, and fancied myself still on Sandpeep Island : now we were building our brick stove to cook the chowder, and, in my delirium, I laughed aloud and shouted to my comrades ; now the sky darkened, and the squall struck the island ; now I gave orders to Wallace how to manage the boat, and now I cried because the rain was pouring in on me through the holes in the tent. Towards evening a high fever set in, and it was many days before my grandfather deemed it prudent to tell me that the Dolphin had been found, floating keel upwards, four miles southeast of Mackerel Reef.

Poor little Binny Wallace! How strange it seemed, when I went to school again, to see that empty seat in the fifth row ! How gloomy the playground was, lacking the sunshine of his gentle, sensitive face! One day a folded sheet slipped from my algebra ; it was the last note he ever wrote me. I could not read it for the tears.

What a pang shot across my heart the afternoon it was whispered through the town that a body had been washed ashore at Grave Point — the place where we bathed. We bathed there no more ! How well I remember the funeral, and what a piteous sight it was afterwards to see his familiar name on a small headstone in the Old South Burying Ground!

Poor little Binny Wallace! Always the same to me. The rest of us have grown up into hard, worldly men, fighting the fight of life; but you are forever young, and gentle, and pure; a part of my own childhood that time cannot wither; always a little boy, always poor little Binny Wallace!

CHAPTER XV

AN OLD ACQUAINTANCE TURNS UP

A YEAR had stolen by since the death of Binny Wallace — a year of which I have nothing important to record.

The loss of our little playmate threw a shadow over our young lives for many and many a month. The Dolphin rose and fell with the tide at the foot of the slippery steps, unused, the rest of the summer. At the close of November we hauled her sadly into the boathouse for the winter; but when spring came round we launched the Dolphin again, and often went down to the wharf and looked at her lying in the tangled eelgrass, without much inclination to take a row. The associations connected with the boat were too painful as yet; but time, which wears the sharp edge from everything, softened this feeling, and one afternoon we brought out the cobwebbed oars.

The ice once broken, brief trips along the wharves — we seldom cared to go out into the river now — became one of our chief amusements. Meanwhile Gypsy was not forgotten. Every clear morning I was in the saddle before breakfast, and there are few roads or lanes within ten miles of

Rivermouth that have not borne the print of her vagrant hoof.

I studied like a good fellow this quarter, carrying off a couple of first prizes. The Captain expressed his gratification by presenting me with a new silver dollar. If a dollar in his eyes was smaller than a cart-wheel, it was not so very much smaller. I redeemed my pencil-case from the treasurer of the Centipedes, and felt that I was getting on in the world

It was at this time I was greatly cast down by a letter from my father saying that he should be unable to visit Rivermouth until the following year. With that letter came another to Captain Nutter, which he did not read aloud to the family, as usual. It was on business, he said, folding it up in his wallet. He received several of these business letters from time to time, and I noticed that they always made him silent and moody.

The fact is my father's banking-house was not thriving. The unlooked-for failure of a firm largely indebted to him had crippled "the house." When the Captain imparted this information to me I did not trouble myself over the matter. I supposed — if I supposed anything — that all grown-up people had more or less money, when they wanted it. Whether they inherited it, or whether government supplied them, was not clear to me. A loose idea that my father had a private gold-mine somewhere or other relieved me of all uneasiness.

I was not far from right. Every man has within himself a gold-mine whose riches are limited only by his own industry. It is true, it sometimes happens that industry does not avail, if a man lacks that something which, for want of a better name, we call luck. My father was a person of untiring energy and ability ; but he had no luck. To use a Rivermouth saying, he was always catching sculpins when every one else with the same bait was catching mackerel.

It was more than two years since I had seen my parents. I felt that I could not bear a longer separation. Every letter from New Orleans — we got two or three a month — gave me a fit of home-sickness ; and when it was definitely settled that my father and mother were to remain in the South another twelvemonth, I resolved to go to them.

Since Binny Wallace's death, Pepper Whitcomb had been my *fidus Achates ;* we occupied desks near each other at school, and were always together in play hours. We rigged a twine telegraph from his garret window to the scuttle of the Nut-ter House, and sent messages to each other in a match-box. We shared our pocket-money and our secrets — those amazing secrets which boys have. We met in lonely places by stealth, and parted like conspirators ; we could not buy a jackknife or build a kite without throwing an air of mystery and guilt over the transaction.

I naturally hastened to lay my New Orleans

project before Pepper Whitcomb, having dragged
him for that purpose to a secluded spot in the
dark pine woods outside the town.   Pepper listened to me with a gravity which he will not be

The Telegraph

able to surpass when he becomes Chief Justice,
and strongly advised me to go.

"The summer vacation," said Pepper, "lasts
six weeks ; that will give you a fortnight to spend
in New Orleans, allowing two weeks each way for
the journey."

I wrung his hand and begged him to accompany
me, offering to defray all the expenses.   I was nothing if I was not princely in those days.   After
considerable urging, he consented to go on terms
so liberal.   The whole thing was arranged ; there
was nothing to do now but to advise Captain Nutter of my plan, which I did the next day.

The possibility that he might oppose the tour never entered my head. I was therefore totally unprepared for the vigorous negative which met my proposal. I was deeply mortified, moreover, for there was Pepper Whitcomb on the wharf, at the foot of the street, waiting for me to come and let him know what day we were to start.

"Go to New Orleans? Go to Jericho!" exclaimed Captain Nutter. "You'd look pretty, you two, philandering off, like the babes in the wood, twenty-five hundred miles, 'with all the world before you where to choose'!"

And the Captain's features, which had worn an indignant air as he began the sentence, relaxed into a broad smile. Whether it was at the felicity of his own quotation, or at the mental picture he drew of Pepper and myself on our travels, I could not tell, and little cared. I was heart-broken. How could I face my chum after all the dazzling inducements I had held out to him?

My grandfather, seeing that I took the matter seriously, pointed out the difficulties of such a journey and the great expense involved. He entered into the details of my father's money troubles, and succeeded in making it plain to me that my wishes, under the circumstances, were somewhat unreasonable. It was in no cheerful mood that I joined Pepper at the end of the wharf.

I found that young gentleman leaning against the bulkhead gazing intently towards the islands

in the harbor.   He had formed a telescope of his
hands, and was so occupied with his observations
as to be oblivious of my approach.

"Hullo!" cried Pepper, dropping his hands.
"Look there! is n't that a bark coming up the
Narrows?"

"Where?"

"Just at the left of Fishcrate Island.   Don't
you see the foremast peeping above the old der-
rick?"

Sure enough, it was a vessel of considerable size,
slowly beating up to town.   In a few moments
more the other two masts were visible above the
green hillocks.

"Fore-topmasts blown away," said Pepper.
"Putting in for repairs, I guess."

As the bark lazily crept from behind the last of
the islands, she let go her anchors and swung
round with the tide.   Then the gleeful chant of
the sailors at the capstan came to us pleasantly
across the water.   The vessel lay within three
quarters of a mile of us, and we could plainly see
the men at the davits lowering the starboard
long-boat.   It no sooner touched the stream than
a dozen of the crew scrambled like mice over the
side of the merchantman.

In a neglected seaport like Rivermouth the arrival of a large ship is an event of moment.   The
prospect of having twenty or thirty jolly tars let
loose on the peaceful town excites divers emo-

tions among the inhabitants. The small shop-
keepers along the wharves anticipate a thriving
trade ; the proprietors of the two rival boarding-
houses — the " Wee Drop " and the " Mariner's
Home " — hasten down to the landing to secure
lodgers ; and the female population of Anchor
Lane turn out to a woman, for a ship fresh from
sea is always full of possible husbands and long-
lost prodigal sons.

But aside from this there is scant welcome
given to a ship's crew in Rivermouth. The toil-
worn mariner is a
sad fellow ashore,
judging him by
a severe moral
standard.

Once, I re-
member, a Unit-
ed States frigate
came into port for
repairs after a
storm. She lay
in the river a fort-
night or more,

A Midnight Call

and every day
sent us a gang of sixty or seventy of our country's
gallant defenders, who spread themselves over the
town, doing all sorts of mad things. They were
good-natured enough, but full of old Sancho.
The " Wee Drop " proved a drop too much for

many of them.   They went singing through the
streets at midnight, wringing off door-knockers,
shinning up water-spouts, and frightening the Oldest Inhabitant nearly to death by popping their
heads into his second-story window, and shouting
"Fire!"   One morning a blue-jacket was discovered in a perilous plight, half way up the steeple
of the South Church, clinging to the lightning-rod.
How he got there nobody could tell, not even blue-
jacket himself.   All he knew was, that the leg of
his trousers had caught on a nail, and there he
stuck, unable to move either way.   It cost the
town five or six dollars to get him down again.   He
directed the workmen how to splice the ladders
brought to his assistance, and called his rescuers
"butter-fingered land-lubbers" with delicious coolness.

But those were man-of-war's men.   The sedate-
looking craft now lying off Fishcrate Island was
not likely to carry any such lively cargo.   Nevertheless, we watched the coming in of the long-
boat with considerable interest.

As it drew near, the figure of the man pulling
the bow-oar seemed oddly familiar to me.   Where
could I have seen him before?   When and where?
His back was towards me, but there was something about that closely cropped head that I recognized instantly.

"Way enough!" cried the steersman, and all
the oars stood upright in the air.   The man in

the bow seized the boat-hook, and, turning round quickly, showed me the honest face of Sailor Ben of the Typhoon.

"It's Sailor Ben!" I cried, nearly pushing Pepper Whitcomb overboard in my excitement.

Sailor Ben, with the wonderful pink lady on his arm, and the ships and stars and anchors tattooed all over him, was a well-known hero among my playmates. And there he was, like something in a dream come true!

I did not wait for my old acquaintance to get firmly on the wharf, before I grasped his hand in both of mine.

"Sailor Ben, don't you remember me?"

He evidently did not. He shifted his quid from one cheek to the other, and looked at me meditatively.

"Lord love ye, lad, I don't know you. I was never here afore in my life."

"What!" I cried, enjoying his perplexity, "have you forgotten the voyage from New Orleans in the Typhoon, two years ago, you lovely old picture-book?"

Ah! then he knew me, and in token of the recollection gave my hand such a squeeze that I am sure an unpleasant change came over my countenance.

"Bless my eyes, but you have growed! I should n't have knowed you if I had met you in Singapore!"

Without stopping to inquire, as I was tempted to do, why he was more likely to recognize me in Singapore than anywhere else, I invited him to come at once up to the Nutter House, where I insured him a warm welcome from the Captain.

"Hold steady, Master Tom," said Sailor Ben, slipping the painter through the ringbolt and tying the loveliest knot you ever saw ; "hold steady till I see if the mate can let me off.   If you please, sir," he continued, addressing the steersman, a very red-faced, bow-legged person, "this here is a little shipmate o' mine as wants to talk over back times along of me, if so it 's convenient."

"All right, Ben," returned the mate; "shan't want you for an hour."

Leaving one man in charge of the boat, the mate and the rest of the crew went off together. In the mean while Pepper Whitcomb had got out his cunner line, and was quietly fishing at the end of the wharf, as if to give me the idea that he was not very much impressed by my intimacy with so renowned a character as Sailor Ben.   Perhaps Pepper was a little jealous.   At any rate, he refused to go with us to the house.

Captain Nutter was at home reading the Rivermouth Barnacle.   He was a reader to do an editor's heart good ; he never skipped over an advertisement, even if he had read it fifty times before. Then the paper went the rounds of the neighborhood, among the poor people, like the single portable eye which the three blind crones passed to each other in the legend of King Acrisius. The Captain, I repeat, was wandering in the labyrinths of the Rivermouth Barnacle when I led Sailor Ben into the sitting-room.

My grandfather, whose inborn courtesy knew no distinctions, received my nautical friend as if he had been an admiral instead of a common fore-castle-hand. Sailor Ben pulled an imaginary tuft of hair on his forehead, and bowed clumsily. Sailors have a way of using their forelock as a sort of handle to bow with.

The old tar had probably never been in so handsome an apartment in all his days, and nothing could induce him to take the inviting mahogany chair which the Captain wheeled out from the corner.

The abashed mariner stood up against the wall, twirling his tarpaulin in his two hands and looking extremely silly. He made a poor show in a gentleman's drawing-room, but what a fellow he had been in his day, when the gale blew great guns and the topsails wanted reefing! I thought of him with the Mexican squadron off Vera Cruz, where

" The rushing battle-bolt sung from the three-decker out of the foam,"

and he did not seem awkward or ignoble to me, for all his shyness.

As Sailor Ben declined to sit down, the Captain

did not resume his seat ; so we three stood in a constrained manner until my grandfather went to the door and called to Kitty to bring in a decanter of madeira and two glasses.

"My grandson, here, has talked so much about

Introducing Sailor Ben

you," said the Captain pleasantly, "that you seem quite like an old acquaintance to me."

"Thankee, sir, thankee," returned Sailor Ben, looking as guilty as if he had been detected in picking a pocket.

"And I 'm very glad to see you, Mr. — Mr. — "

"Watson — Benjamin Watson."

"Mr. Watson," added the Captain.   "Tom, open the door, there 's Kitty with the glasses."

I opened the door, and Kitty entered the room bringing the things on a waiter, which she was about to set on the table, when suddenly she uttered a loud shriek; the decanter and glasses fell with a crash to the floor, and Kitty, as white as a sheet, was seen flying through the hall.

"It 's his wraith!   It 's his wraith [1]!" we heard Kitty shrieking, in the kitchen.

My grandfather and I turned with amazement to Sailor Ben.   His eyes were standing out of his head like a lobster's.

"It 's my own little Irish lass!" shouted the sailor, and he darted into the hall after her.

Even then we scarcely caught the meaning of his words, but when we saw Watson and Kitty sobbing on each other's shoulder in the kitchen, we understood it all.

"I begs your honor's parden, sir," he said, lifting his tear-stained face above Kitty's tumbled hair ; "I begs your honor's parden for kicking up a rumpus in the house, but it 's my own little Irish lass as I lost so long ago !"

"Heaven preserve us !" cried the Captain, blowing his nose violently — a transparent ruse to hide his emotion.

[1] Ghost, spirit.

Miss Abigail was in an upper chamber, sweeping ; but on hearing the unusual racket below, she scented an accident and came ambling downstairs with a bottle of the infallible hot-drops in her hand. Nothing but the firmness of my grandfather prevented her from giving Sailor Ben a tablespoonful on the spot. But when she learned what had come about — that this was Kitty's husband, that Kitty Collins was not Kitty Collins now, but Mrs. Benjamin Watson of Nantucket — the good soul sat down on the meal-chest and sobbed as if — to quote from Captain Nutter — as if a husband of her own had turned up !

A happier set of persons than we were never met together in a dingy kitchen or anywhere else. The Captain ordered a fresh decanter of madeira, and made all hands, excepting myself, drink a cup to the return of " the prodigal sea-son," as he called Sailor Ben.

After the first flush of joy and surprise was over, Kitty grew silent and constrained.   Now and then she fixed her eyes thoughtfully on her husband. Why had he deserted her all these long years ? What right had he to look for a welcome from one he had treated so cruelly ? She had been true to him, but had he been true to her ? Sailor Ben must have guessed what was passing in her mind, for presently he took her hand and said, —

" Well, lass, it 's a long yarn, but you shall have it all in good time.   It was my hard luck as made us part company, an' no will of mine, for I loved you dear."

Kitty brightened up immediately, needing no other assurance of Sailor Ben's faithfulness.

When his hour had expired, we walked with him down to the wharf, where the Captain held a consultation with the mate, which resulted in an extension of Mr. Watson's leave of absence, and afterwards in his discharge from his ship. We then went to the "Mariner's Home" to engage a room for him, as he would not hear of accepting the hospitalities of the Nutter House.

"You see, I 'm only an uneddicated man," he remarked to my grandfather, by way of explanation.

CHAPTER XVI

OF course we were all very curious to learn what had befallen Sailor Ben that morning long ago, when he bade his little bride good-by and disappeared so mysteriously.

After tea, that same evening, we assembled around the table in the kitchen — the only place where Sailor Ben felt at home — to hear what he had to say for himself.

The candles were snuffed, and a pitcher of foaming nut-brown ale was set at the elbow of the speaker, who was evidently embarrassed by the respectability of his audience, consisting of Captain Nutter, Miss Abigail, myself, and Kitty, whose face shone with happiness like one of the polished tin platters on the dresser.

" Well, my hearties," commenced Sailor Ben — then he stopped short and turned very red, as it struck him that maybe this was not quite the proper way to address a dignitary like the Captain and a severe elderly lady like Miss Abigail Nutter, who sat bolt upright staring at him as she would have stared at the Tycoon of Japan himself.

" I ain't much of a hand at spinnin' a yarn,"

remarked Sailor Ben, apologetically, " 'specially when the yarn is all about a man as has made a fool of hisself, an' 'specially when that man's name is Benjamin Watson."

"Bravo!" cried Captain Nutter, rapping on the table encouragingly.

"Thankee, sir, thankee. I go back to the time when Kitty an' me was livin' in lodgin's by the dock in New York. We was as happy, sir, as two porpusses, which they toil not neither do they spin. But when I seed the money gittin' low in the locker — Kitty's starboard stockin', savin' your presence, marm — I got down-hearted like, seein' as I should be obleeged to skip agin, for it did n't seem as I could do much ashore. An' then the sea was my nat'ral spear of action. I was n't exactly born on it, look you, but I fell into it the fust time I was let out arter my birth. My mother slipped her cable for a heavenly port afore I was old enough to hail her; so I larnt to look on the ocean for a sort of stepmother — an' a precious hard one she has been to me.

"The idee of leavin' Kitty so soon arter our marriage went agin my grain considerable. I cruised along the docks for somethin' to do in the way of stevedore ; an' though I picked up a stray job here and there, I did n't arn enough to buy ship-bisket for a rat, let alone feedin' two human mouths. There was n't nothin' honest I would n't have turned a hand to ; but the 'longshoremen gobbled up all the work, an' a outsider like me did n't stand a show.

"Things got from bad to worse ; the month's rent took all our cash except a dollar or so, an' the sky looked kind o' squally fore an' aft. Well, I set out one mornin' — that identical unlucky mornin' — determined to come back an' toss some pay into Kitty's lap, if I had to sell my jacket for it. I spied a brig unloadin' coal at pier No. 47 — how well I remembers it ! I hailed the mate, an' offered myself for a coal-heaver. But I was n't wanted, as he told me civilly enough, which was better treatment than usual. As I turned off rather glum I was signaled by one of them sleek, smooth-spoken rascals with a white hat an' a weed on it, as is always goin' about the piers a-seekin' who they may devower.

"We sailors know 'em for rascals from stem to starn, but somehow every fresh one fleeces us jest as his mate did afore him. We don't larn nothin' by exper'ence ; we're jest no better than a lot of babbys with no brains.

" ' Good-mornin', my man,' sez the chap, as iley as you please.

" ' Mornin', sir,' sez I.

" ' Lookin' for a job ? ' sez he.

" ' Through the big end of a telescope,' sez I — meanin' that the chances for a job looked very small from my pint of view.

" ' You 're the man for my money,' sez he

smilin' as innocent as a cherubim ; 'jest step in here, till we talk it over.'

"So I goes with him like a nat'ral-born idiot, into a little grocery-shop near by, where we sets down at a table with a bottle atween us.   Then it comes out as there is a New Bedford whaler about

" Lookin' for a job ? "

to start for the fishin' grounds, an' jest one able-bodied sailor like me is wanted to make up the crew.   Would I go?   Yes, I would n't on no terms.

"'I'll bet you fifty dollars,' sez he, 'that you'll come back fust mate.'

"'I'll bet you a hundred,' sez I, 'that I don't,

for I 've signed papers as keeps me ashore, an' the parson has witnessed the deed.'

" So we sat there, he urgin' me to ship, an' I chaffin' him cheerful over the bottle.

" Arter a while I begun to feel a little queer ; things got foggy in my upper works, an' I remembers, faintlike, of signin' a paper ; then I remembers bein' in a small boat ; and then I remembers nothin' until I heard the mate's whistle pipin' all hands on deck. I tumbled up with the rest, an' there I was — on board of a whaler outward bound for a three years' cruise, an' my dear little lass ashore awaitin' for me."

" Miserable wretch !" said Miss Abigail, in a voice that vibrated among the tin platters on the dresser. This was Miss Abigail's way of testifying her sympathy.

" Thankee, marm," returned Sailor Ben doubtfully.

" No talking to the man at the wheel," cried the Captain. Upon which we all laughed. " Spin !" added my grandfather.

Sailor Ben resumed : —

" I leave you to guess the wretchedness as fell upon me, for I 've not got the gift to tell you. There I was down on the ship's books for a three years' viage, an' no help for it. I feel nigh to six hundred years old when I think how long that viage was. There is n't no hour-glass as runs slow enough to keep a tally of the slowness of them

fust hours. But I done my duty like a man, seein'
there was n't no way of gettin' out of it. I told
my shipmates of the trick as had been played on
me, an' they tried to cheer me up a bit; but I was
sore sorrowful for a long spell. Many a night on
watch I put my face in my hands and sobbed for
thinkin' of the little woman left among the land-
sharks, an' no man to have an eye on her, God
bless her!"

Here Kitty softly drew her chair nearer to
Sailor Ben, and rested one hand on his arm.

"Our adventures among the whales, I take it,
does n't consarn the present company here assembled. So I give that the go by. There 's an end
to everythin', even to a whalin' viage. My heart
all but choked me the day we put into New Bedford with our cargo of ile. I got my three years'
pay in a lump, an' made for New York like a
flash of lightnin'. The people hove to and looked
at me, as I rushed through the streets like a madman, until I came to the spot where the lodgin'-
house stood on West Street. But, Lord love ye,
there was no sech lodgin'-house there, but a great
new brick shop.

"I made bold to go in an' ask arter the old
place, but nobody knowed nothin' about it, save as
it had been torn down two years or more. I *was*
adrift now, for I had reckoned all them days and
nights on gittin' word of Kitty from Dan Shackford, the man as kept the lodgin'.

"As I stood there with all the wind knocked
out of my sails, the idee of runnin' alongside the
perlice-station popped into my head.   The perlice
was likely to know the latitude of a man like Dan

Settling the Land Shark's Account

Shackford who was n't over an' above respeck-
tible.   They did know — he had died in the
Tombs jail that day twelvemonth.   A coincydunce, was n't it ?   I was ready to drop when
they told me this ; howsomever, I bore up an' give
the chief a notion of the fix I was in.   He writ a
notice which I put into the newspapers every day

for three months; but nothin' come of it. I
cruised over the city week in and week out; I
went to every sort of place where they hired women hands; I did n't leave a think undone that
a uneddicated man could do. But nothin' come
of it. I don't believe there was a wretcheder
soul in that big city of wretchedness than me.
Sometimes I wanted to lay down in the streets
and die.

"Driftin' disconsolate one day among the ship-
pin', who should I overhaul but the identical
smooth-spoken chap with a white hat an' a weed
on it! I did n't know if there was any sperit left
in me, till I clapped eye on his very onpleasant
countenance. 'You villain!' sez I, 'where's my
little Irish lass as you dragged me away from?'
an' I lighted on him, hat and all, like that!"

Here Sailor Ben brought his fist down on the
deal table with the force of a sledge-hammer.
Miss Abigail gave a start, and the ale leaped up
in the pitcher like a miniature fountain.

"I begs your parden, ladies and gentlemen;
but the thought of that feller with his ring an'
his watch-chain an' his walrus face is alus too
many for me. I was for pitchin' him into the
North River, when a perliceman prevented me
from benefitin' the human family. I had to pay
five dollars for hitin' the chap (they said it was salt
and buttery), an' that's what I call a neat, genteel
luxury. It was worth double the money jest to

see that white hat, with a weed on it, layin' on the wharf like a busted accordiun.

"Arter months of useless sarch, I went to sea agin. I never got into a foren port but I kept a watch out for Kitty. Once I thought I seed her in Liverpool, but it was only a gal as looked like her. The numbers of women in different parts of the world as looked like her was amazin'. So a good many years crawled by, an' I wandered from place to place, never givin' up the sarch. I might have been chief mate scores of times, maybe master ; but I had n't no ambition. I seed many strange things in them years — outlandish people an' cities, storms, shipwracks, an' battles. I seed many a true mate go down, an' sometimes I envied them what went to their rest. But these things is neither here nor there.

"About a year ago I shipped on board the Belphœbe yonder, an' of all the strange winds as ever blowed, the strangest an' the best was the wind as blowed me to this here blessed spot. I can't be too thankful. That I 'm as thankful as it is possible for an uneddicated man to be, He knows as reads the heart of all."

Here ended Sailor Ben's yarn, which I have written down in his own homely words as nearly as I can recall them. After he had finished, the Captain shook hands with him and served out the ale.

As Kitty was about to drink, she paused, rested

the cup on her knee, and asked what day of the month it was.

"The twenty-seventh," said the Captain, wondering what she was driving at.

"Then," cried Kitty, "it's ten years and a day this night sence" —

"Since what ?" asked my grandfather.

"Sence the little woman and I got spliced!" cried Sailor Ben. "There's another coincydunce for you, if you 're wanting anything in that line."

On hearing this we all clapped hands, and the Captain, with a degree of ceremony that was almost painful, drank a bumper to the health and happiness of the bride and bridegroom.

It was a pleasant sight to see the two old lovers sitting side by side, in spite of all, drinking from the same little cup — a battered zinc dipper which Sailor Ben had unslung from a strap round his waist. I think I never saw him without this dipper and a sheath-knife suspended just back of his hip, ready for any convivial occasion.

We had a merry time of it. The Captain was in great force this evening, and not only related his famous exploit in the war of 1812, but regaled the company with a dashing sea-song from Mr. Shakespeare's play of The Tempest. My grandfather — however it came about — was a great reader of Shakespeare. He had a mellow tenor voice (not Shakespeare, but the Captain), and rolled out the verse with a will :

"The master, the swabber, the boatswain, and I,
   The gunner, and his mate,
  Lov'd Mall, Meg, and Marian, and Margery,
   But none of us car'd for Kate."

"A very good song, and very well sung," says Sailor Ben; "but some of us *does* care for Kate. Is this Mr. Shawkspear a sea-farin' man, sir?"

"Not at present," replied the Captain, with a monstrous twinkle in his eye.

The clock was striking ten when the party broke up. The Captain walked to the "Mariner's Home" with his guest, in order to question him regarding his future movements.

"Well, sir," said he, "I ain't as young as I was, an' I don't cal'ulate to go to sea no more. I proposes to drop anchor here, an' hug the land until the old hulk goes to pieces. I've got two or three thousand dollars in the locker, an' expects to get on uncommon comfortable without askin' no odds from the Assylum for Decayed Mariners."

My grandfather indorsed the plan warmly, and Benjamin Watson did drop anchor in Rivermouth, where he speedily became one of the institutions of the town.

His first step was to buy a small one-story cottage located at the head of the wharf, within gunshot of the Nutter House. To the great amusement of my grandfather, Sailor Ben painted the cottage a light sky-blue, and ran a broad black stripe around it just under the eaves. In this stripe he painted white port-holes, at regular distances, making his residence look as much like a man-of-war as possible. With a short flagstaff projecting over the door like a bowsprit, the effect was quite magical. My description of the exterior of this palatial residence is complete when I add that the proprietor nailed a horseshoe against the front door to keep off the witches — a very necessary precaution in these latitudes.

The inside of Sailor Ben's abode was not less striking than the outside. The cottage contained two rooms; the one opening on the wharf he called his cabin; here he ate and slept. His few tumblers and a frugal collection of crockery were set in a rack suspended over the table, which had a cleat of wood nailed round the edge to prevent the dishes from sliding off in case of a heavy sea. Hanging against the walls were three or four highly colored prints of celebrated frigates, and a lithograph picture of a rosy young woman insufficiently clad in the American flag. This was labeled " Kitty," though I am sure it looked no more like her than I did. A walrus-tooth with an Esquimau engraved on it, a shark's jaw, and the blade of a swordfish were among the enviable decorations of this apartment. In one corner stood his bunk, or bed, and in the other his well-worn sea-chest, a perfect Pandora's box of mysteries. You would have thought yourself in the cabin of a real ship.

In the Cabin

The little room aft, separated from the cabin by a sliding door, was the caboose. It held a cooking-stove, pots, pans, and groceries ; also a lot of fishing-lines and coils of tarred twine, which made the place smell like a forecastle, and a delightful smell it is — to those who fancy it.

Kitty did not leave our service, but played housekeeper for both establishments, returning at night to Sailor Ben's. He shortly added a wherry to his worldly goods, and in the fishing season made a very handsome income. During the winter he employed himself manufacturing crab-nets, for which he found no lack of customers.

His popularity among the boys was immense. A jackknife in his expert hand was a whole chest of tools. He could whittle out anything from a wooden chain to a Chinese pagoda, or a full-rigged seventy-four a foot long. To own a ship of Sailor Ben's building was to be exalted above your fellow-creatures. He did not carve many, and those he refused to sell, choosing to present them to his young friends, of whom Tom Bailey, you may be sure, was one.

How delightful it was of winter nights to sit in his cosy cabin, close to the ship's stove (he would never hear of having a fireplace), and listen to Sailor Ben's yarns! In the early summer twilights, when he sat on the door-step splicing a rope or mending a net, he always had a bevy of blooming young faces alongside.

The dear old fellow! How tenderly the years touched him after this! — all the more tenderly, it seemed, for having roughed him so cruelly in other days.

CHAPTER XVII

SAILOR BEN's arrival partly drove the New Orleans project from my brain. Besides, there was just then a certain movement on foot by the Centipede Club which helped to engross my attention.

Pepper Whitcomb took the Captain's veto philosophically, observing that he thought from the first the governor would not let me go. I do not think Pepper was quite honest in that.

But to the subject in hand.

Among the few changes that have taken place in Rivermouth during the past twenty years there is one which I regret. I lament the removal of all those varnished iron cannon which used to do duty as posts at the corners of streets leading from the river. They were quaintly ornamental, each set upon end with a solid shot soldered into its mouth, and gave to that part of the town a picturesqueness very poorly atoned for by the conventional wooden stakes that have deposed them.

These guns ("old sogers" the boys called them) had their story, like everything else in Rivermouth. When that everlasting last war — the war of 1812, I mean — came to an end, all the brigs,

schooners, and barks fitted out at this port as privateers were as eager to get rid of their useless
twelve-pounders and swivels as they had previously been to obtain them. Many of the pieces
had cost large sums, and now they were little better than so much crude iron — not so good, in fact,
for they were clumsy things to break up and melt
over. The government did not want them; private citizens did not want them; they were a drug
in the market.

But there was one man, ridiculous beyond his
generation, who got it into his head that a fortune
was to be made out of these same guns. To buy
them all, to hold on to them until war was declared
again (as he had no doubt it would be in a few
months), and then sell out at fabulous prices —
this was the daring idea that addled the pate of
Silas Trefethen, "Dealer in E. & W. I. Goods
and Groceries," as the faded sign over his shop-
door informed the public.

Silas went shrewdly to work, buying up every
old cannon he could lay hands on. His back yard
was soon crowded with broken-down gun-car-
riages, and his barn with guns, like an arsenal.
When Silas's purpose got wind it was astonishing
how valuable that thing became which just now
was worth nothing at all.

"Ha, ha!" thought Silas; "somebody else is
tryin' tu git control of the market. But I guess
I 've got the start of *him*."

So he went on buying and buying, oftentimes paying double the original price of the article. People in the neighboring towns collected all the worthless ordnance they could find, and sent it by the cart-load to Rivermouth.

When his barn was full, Silas began piling the rubbish in his cellar, then in his parlor. He mortgaged the stock of his grocery-store, mortgaged his house, his barn, his horse, and would have mortgaged himself if any one would have taken him as security, in order to carry on the grand speculation. He was a ruined man, and as happy as a lark.

Surely poor Silas was cracked, like the majority of his own cannon. More or less crazy he must have been always. Years before this he purchased an elegant rosewood coffin, and kept it in one of the spare rooms in his residence. He even had his name engraved on the silver-plate, leaving a blank after the word " Died."

The blank was filled up in due time, and well it was for Silas that he secured so stylish a coffin in his opulent days, for when he died his worldly wealth would not have bought him a pine box, to say nothing of rosewood. He never gave up expecting a war with Great Britain. Hopeful and radiant to the last, his dying words were, *England — war — few days — great profits !*

It was that sweet old lady, Dame Jocelyn, who told me the story of Silas Trefethen ; for these things happened long before my day. Silas died in 1817.

At Trefethen's death his unique collection came under the auctioneer's hammer. Some of the larger guns were sold to the town, and planted at the corners of divers streets; others went off to the iron-foundry; the balance, numbering twelve, were dumped down on a deserted wharf at the foot of Anchor Lane, where, summer after summer, they rested at their ease in the grass and fungi, pelted in autumn by the rain and annually buried by the winter snow. It is with these twelve guns that our story has to deal.

The wharf where they reposed was shut off from the street by a high fence — a silent, dreamy old wharf, covered with strange weeds and mosses. On account of its seclusion and the good fishing it afforded, it was much frequented by us boys.

There we met many an afternoon to throw out our lines, or play leap-frog among the rusty cannon. They were famous fellows in our eyes. What a racket they had made in the heyday of their unchastened youth! What stories they might tell now, if their puffy metallic lips could only speak! Once they were lively talkers enough; but there the grim sea-dogs lay, silent and forlorn in spite of all their former growlings.

They always seemed to me like a lot of venerable disabled tars, stretched out on a lawn in front of a hospital, gazing seaward, and mutely lamenting their lost youth.

But once more they were destined to lift up their dolorous voices — once more they keeled over and lay speechless for all time. And this is how it befell.

Jack Harris, Charley Marden, Harry Blake, and myself were fishing off the wharf one afternoon, when a thought flashed upon me like an inspiration.

"I say, boys!" I cried, hauling in my line hand over hand, "I 've got something!"

"What does it pull like, youngster?" asked Harris, looking down at the taut line and expecting to see a big perch at least.

"Oh, nothing in the fish way," I returned, laughing; "it 's about the old guns."

"What about them?"

"I was thinking what jolly fun it would be to set one of the old sogers on his legs and serve him out a ration of gunpowder."

Up came the three lines in a jiffy. An enterprise better suited to the disposition of my companions could not have been proposed.

In a short time we had one of the smaller cannon over on its back and were busy scraping the green rust from the touch-hole. The mould had spiked the gun so effectually, that for a while we fancied we should have to give up our attempt to resuscitate the old soger.

"A long gimlet would clear it out," said Charley Marden, "if we only had one."

Cleaning Her Out

I looked to see if Sailor Ben's flag was flying at the cabin door, for he always took in the colors when he went off fishing.

"When you want to know if the Admiral's aboard, jest cast an eye to the buntin', my hearties," says Sailor Ben.

Sometimes in a jocose mood he called himself the Admiral, and I am sure he deserved to be one. The Admiral's flag was flying, and I soon procured a gimlet from his carefully kept tool-chest.

Before long we had the gun in working order. A newspaper lashed to the end of a lath served as a swab to dust out the bore. Jack Harris blew through the touch-hole and pronounced all clear.

Seeing our task accomplished so easily, we turned our attention to the other guns, which lay in all sorts of postures in the rank grass. Borrowing a rope from Sailor Ben, we managed with immense labor to drag the heavy pieces into position and place a brick under each muzzle to give it the proper elevation. When we beheld them all in a row, like a regular battery, we simultaneously conceived an idea, the magnitude of which struck us dumb for a moment.

Our first intention was to load and fire a single gun. How feeble and insignificant was such a plan compared to that which now sent the light dancing into our eyes!

"What could we have been thinking of?" cried Jack Harris. "We'll give 'em a broadside, to be sure, if we die for it!"

We turned to with a will, and before nightfall had nearly half the battery overhauled and ready for service. To keep the artillery dry we stuffed wads of loose hemp into the muzzles, and fitted wooden pegs to the touch-holes.

At recess the next noon the Centipedes met in a corner of the school-yard to talk over the proposed lark. The original projectors, though they would have liked to keep the thing secret, were obliged to make a club matter of it, inasmuch as funds were required for ammunition. There had been no recent drain on the treasury, and the society could well afford to spend a few dollars in so notable an undertaking.

It was unanimously agreed that the plan should be carried out in the handsomest manner, and a subscription to that end was taken on the spot. Several of the Centipedes had n't a cent, excepting the one strung around their necks; others, however, were richer. I chanced to have a dollar, and it went into the cap quicker than lightning. When the club, in view of my munificence, voted to name the guns Bailey's Battery, I was prouder than I have ever been since over anything.

The money thus raised, added to that already in the treasury, amounted to nine dollars — a fortune in those days; but not more than we had use for. This sum was divided into twelve parts, for it would not do for one boy to buy all the powder, nor even for us all to make our purchases at the same place. That would excite suspicion at any time, particularly at a period so remote from the Fourth of July.

There were only three stores in town licensed to sell powder; that gave each store four customers. Not to run the slightest risk of remark, one boy bought his powder on Monday, the next boy on Tuesday, and so on until the requisite quantity was in our possession. This we put into a keg and carefully hid in a dry spot on the wharf.

Our next step was to finish cleaning the guns, which occupied two afternoons, for several of the old sogers were in a very congested state indeed. Having completed the task, we came upon a difficulty. To set off the battery by daylight was out of the question ; it must be done at night ; it must be done with fuses, for no doubt the neighbors would turn out after the first two or three shots, and it would not pay to be caught in the vicinity.

Who knew anything about fuses ? Who could arrange it so the guns would go off one after the other, with an interval of a minute or so between ?

Theoretically we knew that a minute fuse lasted a minute ; double the quantity, two minutes ; but practically we were at a stand-still. There was but one person who could help us in this extremity — Sailor Ben. To me was assigned the duty of obtaining what information I could from the ex-gunner, it being left to my discretion whether or not to intrust him with our secret.

So one evening I dropped into the cabin and artfully turned the conversation to fuses in general, and then to particular fuses, but without getting much out of the old boy, who was busy making a twine hammock. Finally, I was forced to divulge the whole plot.

The Admiral had a sailor's love for a joke, and entered at once and heartily into our scheme. He volunteered to prepare the fuses himself, and I left the labor in his hands, having bound him by several extraordinary oaths — such as " Hope-I-may-die " and "May I sink first " — not to betray us, come what would.

This was Monday evening. On Wednesday the fuses were ready. That night we were to unmuzzle Bailey's Battery. Mr. Grimshaw saw that something was wrong somewhere, for we were restless and absent-minded in the classes, and the best of us came to grief before the morning session was over. When Mr. Grimshaw announced "Guy Fawkes" as the subject for our next composition, you might have knocked down the Mystic Twelve with a feather.

The coincidence was certainly curious, but when a man has committed, or is about to commit, an offense, a hundred trifles, which would pass unnoticed at another time, seem to point at him with convicting fingers. No doubt Guy Fawkes himself received many a start after he had got his wicked kegs of gunpowder neatly piled up under the House of Lords.

Wednesday, as I have mentioned, was a half-holiday, and the Centipedes assembled in my barn to decide on the final arrangements. These were as simple as could be. As the fuses were connected, it needed but one person to fire the train. Hereupon arose a discussion as to who was the proper person. Some argued that I ought to apply the match, the battery being christened after me, and the main idea, moreover, being mine. Others advocated the claim of Phil Adams as the oldest boy. At last we drew lots for the post of honor.

Twelve slips of folded paper, upon one of which was written "Thou art the man," were placed in a quart measure, and thoroughly shaken ; then each member stepped up and lifted out his destiny. At a given signal we opened our billets. "Thou art the man," said the slip of paper trembling in my fingers. The sweets and anxieties of a leader were mine the rest of the afternoon.

Directly after twilight set in, Phil Adams stole down to the wharf and fixed the fuses to the guns, laying a train of powder from the principal fuse to the fence, through a chink of which I was to drop the match at midnight.

At ten o'clock Rivermouth goes to bed. At eleven o'clock Rivermouth is as quiet as a country churchyard. At twelve o'clock there is nothing left with which to compare the stillness that broods over the little seaport.

In the midst of this stillness I arose and glided out of the house like a phantom bent on an evil errand ; like a phantom I flitted through the silent street, hardly drawing breath until I knelt down beside the fence at the appointed place.

Pausing a moment for my heart to stop thumping, I lighted the match and shielded it with both hands until it was well under way, and then dropped the blazing splinter on the slender thread of gunpowder.

A noiseless flash instantly followed, and all was dark again. I peeped through the crevice in the fence, and saw the main fuse spitting out sparks like a conjurer. Assured that the train had not failed, I took to my heels, fearful lest the fuse might burn more rapidly than we calculated, and cause an explosion before I could get home. This, luckily, did not happen. There is a special Providence that watches over idiots, drunken men, and boys.

I dodged the ceremony of undressing by plunging into bed, jacket, boots, and all. I am not sure I took off my cap ; but I know that I had hardly pulled the coverlid over me, when " Boom ! " sounded the first gun of Bailey's Battery.

I lay as still as a mouse. In less than two minutes there was another burst of thunder, and then another. The third gun was a tremendous fellow and fairly shook the house.

The town was waking up. Windows were thrown open here and there, and people called to each other across the streets asking what that firing was for.

" Boom ! " went gun number four.

I sprung out of bed and tore off my jacket, for I heard the Captain feeling his way along the wall to my chamber. I was half undressed by the time he found the knob of the door.

" I say, sir," I cried, " do you hear those guns ! "

" Not being deaf, I do," said the Captain, a little tartly — any reflection on his hearing always nettled him ; " but what on earth they are for I can't conceive.   You had better get up and dress yourself."

"I'm nearly dressed, sir."

"Boom! Boom!"— two of the guns had gone off together.

The door of Miss Abigail's bedroom opened hastily, and that pink of maidenly propriety stepped out into the hall in her night-gown — the only indecorous thing I ever knew her to do. She held a light-

Miss Abigail awakes

ed candle in her hand and looked like a very aged Lady Macbeth.

"O Dan'el, this is dreadful! What do you suppose it means?"

"I really can't suppose," said the Captain, rubbing his ear ; "but I guess it's over now."

"Boom!" said Bailey's Battery.

Rivermouth was wide awake now, and half the male population were in the streets, running different ways, for the firing seemed to proceed from opposite points of the town.   Everybody waylaid everybody else with questions ; but as no one knew what was the occasion of the tumult, people who were not usually nervous began to be oppressed by the mystery.

Some thought the town was being bombarded; some thought the world was coming to an end, as the pious and ingenious Mr. Miller had recently predicted it would; but those who could not form any theory whatever were the most perplexed.

In the mean while Bailey's Battery bellowed

Bailey's Battery booming

away at regular intervals. The greatest confusion reigned everywhere by this time. People with lanterns rushed hither and thither. The town-watch had turned out to a man, and marched off, in admirable order, in the wrong direction. Discovering their mistake, they retraced their steps, and got down to the wharf just as the last cannon belched forth its lightning.

A dense cloud of sulphurous smoke floated over Anchor Lane, obscuring the starlight. Two or three hundred persons, in various stages of excitement, crowded about the upper end of the wharf, not liking to advance farther until they were satisfied that the explosions were over. A board was here and there blown from the fence, and through the openings thus afforded a few of the more daring spirits at last ventured to crawl.

The cause of the racket soon transpired. A suspicion that they had been sold gradually dawned on the Rivermouthians. Many were exceedingly indignant, and declared that no penalty was severe enough for those concerned in such a prank; others — and these were the very persons who had been terrified nearly out of their wits — had the assurance to laugh, saying that they knew all along it was only a trick.

The town-watch boldly took possession of the ground, and the crowd began to disperse. Knots of gossips lingered here and there near the place, indulging in vain surmises as to who the invisible gunners could be.

There was no more noise that night, but many a timid person lay awake expecting a renewal of the mysterious cannonading. The Oldest Inhabitant refused to go to bed on any terms, but persisted in sitting up in a rocking-chair, with his hat and mittens on, until daybreak.

I thought I should never get to sleep. The moment I drifted off in a doze I fell to laughing and woke myself up. But towards morning slumber overtook me, and I had a series of disagreeable dreams, in one of which I was waited upon by the ghost of Silas Trefethen with an exorbitant bill for the use of his guns. In another, I was dragged before a court-martial and sentenced by Sailor Ben, in a frizzled wig and three-cornered cocked hat, to be shot to death by Bailey's Battery — a sentence which Sailor Ben was about to execute with his own hand, when I suddenly opened my eyes and found the sunshine lying pleasantly across my face. I tell you I was glad!

That unaccountable fascination which leads the guilty to hover about the spot where his crime was committed drew me down to the wharf as soon as I was dressed. Phil Adams, Jack Harris, and others of the conspirators were already there, examining with a mingled feeling of curiosity and apprehension the havoc accomplished by the battery.

The fence was badly shattered and the ground ploughed up for several yards round the place where the guns formerly lay — formerly lay, for now they were scattered every which way. There was scarcely a gun that had not burst. Here was one ripped open from muzzle to breech, and there was another with its mouth blown into the shape of a trumpet. Three of the guns had disappeared bodily, but on looking over the edge of the wharf we saw them standing on end in the tide-mud. They had popped overboard in their excitement.

"I tell you what, fellows," whispered Phil Adams, "it is lucky we did n't try to touch 'em off with punk. They 'd have blown us all to flinders."

The destruction of Bailey's Battery was not, unfortunately, the only catastrophe. A fragment of one of the cannon had carried away the chimney of Sailor Ben's cabin. He was very mad at first, but having prepared the fuse himself he did not dare complain openly.

"I 'd have taken a reef in the blessed stove-pipe," said the Admiral, gazing ruefully at the smashed chimney, "if I had known as how the Flagship was agoin' to be under fire."

The next day he rigged out an iron funnel, which, being in sections, could be detached and taken in at a moment's notice. On the whole, I think he was resigned to the demolition of his brick chimney. The stove-pipe was a great deal more ship-shape.

The town was not so easily appeased. The selectmen determined to make an example of the guilty parties, and offered a reward for their arrest, holding out a promise of pardon to any one

of the offenders who would furnish information
against the rest. But there were no faint hearts
among the Centipedes. Suspicion rested for a
while on several persons — on the soldiers at the
fort ; on a crazy fellow, known about town as
" Bottle-Nose ; " and at last on Sailor Ben.

"Shiver my timbers ! " cries that deeply injured
individual. " Do you suppose, sir, as I have lived
to sixty year, an' ain't got no more sense than
to go for to blaze away at my own upper riggin' ?
It does n't stand to reason."

It certainly did not seem probable that Mr.
Watson would maliciously knock over his own
chimney, and Lawyer Hackett, who had the case
in hand, bowed himself out of the Admiral's cabin,
convinced that the right man had not been discovered.

People living by the sea are always more or less
superstitious. Stories of spectre ships and mysterious beacons, that lure vessels out of their
course and wreck them on unknown reefs, were
among the stock legends of Rivermouth ; and not
a few persons in the town were ready to attribute
the firing of those guns to some supernatural
agency. The Oldest Inhabitant remembered that
when he was a boy a dim-looking sort of
schooner hove to in the offing one foggy afternoon, fired off a single gun that did not make any
report, and then crumbled to nothing, spar, mast,
and hulk, like a piece of burnt paper.

The authorities, however, were of the opinion that human hands had something to do with the explosions, and they resorted to deep-laid stratagems to get hold of the said hands. One of their traps came very near catching us. They artfully caused an old brass fieldpiece to be left on a wharf near the scene of our late operations. Nothing in the world but the lack of money to buy powder saved us from falling into the clutches of the two watchmen who lay secreted for a week in a neighboring sail-loft.

It was many a day before the midnight bombardment ceased to be the town-talk. The trick was so audacious and on so grand a scale that nobody thought for an instant of connecting us lads with it. Suspicion at last grew weary of lighting on the wrong person, and as conjecture — like the physicians in the epitaph — was in vain, the Rivermouthians gave up the idea of finding out who had astonished them.

They never did find out, and never will, unless they read this veracious history. If the selectmen are still disposed to punish the malefactors, I can supply Lawyer Hackett with evidence enough to convict Pepper Whitcomb, Phil Adams, Charley Marden, and the other honorable members of the Centipede Club. But really I do not think it would pay now.

CHAPTER XVIII

A FROG HE WOULD A-WOOING GO

IF the reader supposes that I lived all this while in Rivermouth without falling a victim to one or more of the young ladies attending Miss Dorothy Gibbs's Female Institute, why, then, all I have to say is the reader exhibits his ignorance of human nature.

Miss Gibbs's seminary was located within a few minutes' walk of the Temple Grammar School, and numbered about thirty-five pupils, the majority of whom boarded at the Hall — Primrose Hall, as Miss Dorothy prettily called it. The Primroses, as we called *them*, ranged from seven years of age to sweet seventeen, and a prettier group of sirens never got together even in Rivermouth, for Rivermouth, you should know, is famous for its pretty girls.

There were tall girls and short girls, rosy girls and pale girls, and girls as brown as berries; girls like Amazons, slender girls, weird and winning like Undine, girls with black tresses, girls with auburn ringlets, girls with every tinge of golden hair. To behold Miss Dorothy's young ladies of a Sunday morning walking to church two by two, the smallest toddling at the end of the procession, like the bobs at the tail of a kite, was a spectacle to fill with tender emotion the least susceptible heart. To see Miss Dorothy marching grimly at the head of her light infantry, was to feel the hopelessness of making an attack on any part of the column.

She was a perfect dragon of watchfulness. The most unguarded lifting of an eyelash in the fluttering battalion was sufficient to put her on the lookout. She had had experiences with the male sex, this Miss Dorothy so prim and grim. It was whispered that her heart was a tattered album scrawled over with love-lines, but that she had shut up the volume long ago.

There was a tradition that she had been crossed in love ; but it was the faintest of traditions. A gay young lieutenant of marines had flirted with her at a country ball (A. D. 1811), and then marched carelessly away at the head of his company to the shrill music of the fife, without so much as a sigh for the girl he left behind him. The years rolled on, the gallant gay Lothario — which was not his name — married, became a father, and then a grandfather ; and at the period of which I am speaking his grandchild was actually one of Miss Dorothy's young ladies. So, at least, ran the story.

The lieutenant himself was dead these many years ; but Miss Dorothy never got over his du-

plicity. She was convinced that the sole aim of
mankind was to win the unguarded affection of
maidens, and then march off treacherously with
flying colors to the heartless music of the drum
and fife. To shield the inmates of Primrose Hall
from the bitter influences that had blighted her
own early affections was Miss Dorothy's mission
in life.

"No wolves prowling about my lambs, if you
please," said Miss Dorothy. "I will not allow it."

She was as good as her word. I do not think
the boy lives who ever set foot within the limits
of Primrose Hall while the seminary was under
her charge. Perhaps if Miss Dorothy had given
her young ladies a little more liberty, they would
not have thought it "such fun" to make eyes
over the white lattice fence at the young gentlemen of the Temple Grammar School. I say
perhaps ; for it is one thing to manage thirty-
five young ladies and quite another thing to talk
about it.

But all Miss Dorothy's vigilance could not prevent the young folks from meeting in the town
now and then, nor could her utmost ingenuity interrupt postal arrangements. There was no end
of notes passing between the students and the
Primroses. Notes tied to the heads of arrows
were shot into dormitory windows ; notes were
tucked under fences, and hidden in the trunks of
decayed trees. Every thick place in the boxwood

hedge that surrounded the seminary was a possible post-office.

It was a terrible shock to Miss Dorothy the day she unearthed a nest of letters in one of the huge wooden urns surmounting the gateway that led to her dovecot. It was a bitter moment to Miss Phœbe and Miss Candace and Miss Hesba, when they had their locks of hair grimly handed back to them by Miss Gibbs in the presence of the whole school. Girls whose

The Discovery

locks of hair had run the blockade in safety were particularly severe on the offenders. But it did not stop other notes and other tresses, and I would like to know what can stop them while the earth holds together.

Now when I first came to Rivermouth I looked upon girls as rather tame company; I had not a spark of sentiment concerning them; but seeing my comrades sending and receiving mysterious epistles, wearing bits of ribbon in their button-holes, and leaving packages of confectionery (generally lemon-drops) in the hollow trunks of trees — why, I felt that this was the proper thing to do. I resolved, as a matter of duty, to fall in love with somebody, and I did not care in the least who it was. In much the same mood that Don Quixote selected the Dulcinea del Toboso for his lady-love, I singled out one of Miss Dorothy's incomparable young ladies for mine.

I debated a long while whether I should not select *two*, but at last settled down on one — a pale little girl with blue eyes, named Alice. I shall not make a long story of this, for Alice made short work of me. She was secretly in love with Pepper Whitcomb. This occasioned a temporary coolness between Pepper and myself.

Not disheartened, however, I placed Laura Rice — I believe it was Laura Rice — in the vacant niche. The new idol was more cruel than the old. The former frankly sent me to the right about, but the latter was a deceitful lot. She wore my nosegay in her dress at the evening service (the Primroses were marched to church three times every Sunday), she penned me the daintiest of notes, she sent me the glossiest of ringlets (cut, as I afterwards found out, from the stupid head of Miss Gibbs's chambermaid), and at the same time was holding me and my pony up to ridicule in

a series of letters written to Jack Harris.   It was
Harris himself who kindly opened my eyes.

" I tell you what, Bailey," said that young gentleman, " Laura is an old veteran, and carries too
many guns for a youngster.   She can't resist a
flirtation ; I believe she 'd flirt with an infant in
arms.   There 's hardly a fellow in the school that
has n't worn her colors and some of her hair.
She does n't give out any more of her own hair
now.   She had to stop that.   The demand was
greater than the supply, you see.   It 's all very
well to correspond with Laura, but as to looking
for anything serious from her, the knowing ones
don't.   Hope I have n't hurt your feelings, old
boy " (that was a soothing stroke of flattery to
call me "old boy "), " but 't was my duty as a
friend and a Centipede to let you know who you
were dealing with."

Such was the advice given me by that time-
stricken, careworn, and embittered man of the
world, who was sixteen years old if he was a day.

I dropped Laura.   In the course of the next
twelve months I had perhaps three or four similar
experiences, and the conclusion was forced upon
me that I was not a boy likely to distinguish
myself in this branch of business.

I fought shy of Primrose Hall from that moment.   Smiles were smiled over the boxwood
hedge, and little hands were occasionally kissed to
me ; but I only winked my eye patronizingly, and

passed on. I never renewed tender relations with Miss Gibbs's young ladies. All this occurred during my first year and a half at Rivermouth.

Between my studies at school, my out-door recreations, and the hurts my vanity received, I managed to escape for the time being any very serious attack of that love fever which, like the measles, is almost certain to seize upon a boy sooner or later. I was not to be an exception. I was merely biding my time. The incidents I have now to relate took place shortly after the events described in the last chapter.

In a life so tranquil and circumscribed as ours in the Nutter House, a visitor was a novelty of no little importance. The whole household awoke from its quietude one morning when the Captain announced that a young niece of his from New York was to spend a few weeks with us.

The blue chintz room, into which a ray of sun was never allowed to penetrate, was thrown open and dusted, and its mouldy air made sweet with a bouquet of pot-roses placed on the old-fashioned bureau. Kitty was busy all the forenoon washing off the sidewalk and sand-papering the great brass knocker on our front door ; and Miss Abigail was up to her elbows in a pigeon-pie.

I felt sure it was for no ordinary person that all these preparations were in progress ; and I was right. Miss Nelly Glentworth was no ordinary

person. I shall never believe she was. There
may have been lovelier women, though I have
never seen them; there may have been more
brilliant women, though it has not been my fortune
to meet them; but that there was ever a more
charming one than Nelly Glentworth is a proposition against which I contend.

I do not love her now. I do not think of her
once in five years; and yet it would give me a
turn if in the course of my daily walk I should
suddenly come upon her eldest boy. I may say
that her eldest boy was not playing a prominent
part in this life when I first made her acquaintance.

It was a drizzling, cheerless afternoon towards
the end of summer that a hack drew up at the
door of the Nutter House. The Captain and Miss
Abigail hastened into the hall on hearing the
carriage stop. In a moment more Miss Nelly
Glentworth was seated in our sitting-room under-
going a critical examination at the hands of a
small boy who lounged uncomfortably on a settee
between the windows.

The small boy considered himself a judge of
girls, and he rapidly came to the following conclu-
sions: That Miss Nellie was about nineteen; that
she had not given away much of her back hair,
which hung in two massive chestnut braids over
her shoulders; that she was a shade too pale and
a trifle too tall; that her hands were nicely

shaped and her feet much too diminutive for daily
use. He furthermore observed that her voice was
musical, and that her face lighted up with an in-
describable brightness when she smiled.

On the whole, the small boy liked her well
enough ; and, satisfied that she was not a person
to be afraid of, but, on the contrary, one who
might turn out to be quite agreeable, he departed
to keep an appointment with his friend Sir Pepper
Whitcomb.

But the next morning, when Miss Glentworth
came down to breakfast in a purple dress, her face
as fresh as one of the moss-roses on the bureau
upstairs, and her laugh as contagious as the mer-
riment of a robin, the small boy experienced a
strange sensation, and mentally compared her
with the loveliest of Miss Gibbs's young ladies, and
found those young ladies wanting in the balance.

A night's rest had wrought a wonderful change
in Miss Nelly. The pallor and weariness of the
journey had passed away. I looked at her through
the toast rack and thought I had never seen anything more winning than her smile.

After breakfast she went out with me to the
stable to see Gypsy, and the three of us became
friends then and there. Nelly was the only girl
that Gypsy ever took the slightest notice of.

It chanced to be a half-holiday, and a base-ball
match of unusual interest was to come off on the
school ground that afternoon ; but, somehow, I

did not go.   I hung about the house abstractedly.
The Captain went up town, and Miss Abigail was
busy in the kitchen making immortal gingerbread.
I drifted into the sitting-room, and had our guest
all to myself for I do not know how many hours.
It was twilight, I recollect, when the Captain
returned with letters for Miss Nelly.

Many a time after that I sat with her through
the dreamy September afternoons.   If I had
played base-ball it would have been much better
for me.

Those first days of Miss Nelly's visit are very
misty in my remembrance.   I try in vain to remember just when I began to fall in love with her.
Whether the spell worked upon me gradually or
fell upon me all at once, I do not know.   I only
know that it seemed to me as if I had always
loved her.   Things that took place before she
came were dim to me, like events that had occurred in the Middle Ages.

Nelly was at least five years my senior.   But
what of that ?   Adam is the only man I ever
heard of who did not in early youth fall in love
with a woman older than himself, and I am convinced that he would have done so if he had had
the opportunity.

I wonder if girls from fifteen to twenty are
aware of the glamour they cast over the straggling
awkward boys whom they regard and treat as mere
children.   I wonder, now.   Young women are so

keen in such matters. I wonder if Miss Nelly Glentworth never suspected until the very last night of her visit at Rivermouth that I was over ears in love with her pretty self, and was suffering pangs as poignant as if I had been ten feet high and as old as Methuselah. For, indeed, I was miserable throughout all those five weeks. I went down in the Latin class at the rate of three boys a day. Her fresh young eyes came between me and my book, and there was an end of Virgil

> "O love, love, love!
> Love is like a dizziness,
> It winna let a body
> Gang about his business."

I was wretched away from her, and only less wretched in her presence. The especial cause of my woe was this : I was simply a little boy to Miss Glentworth. I knew it. I bewailed it. I ground my teeth and wept in secret over the fact. If I had been aught else in her eyes would she have smoothed my hair so carelessly, sending an electric shock through my whole system ? would she have walked with me, hand in hand, for hours in the old garden ? and once when I lay on the sofa, my head aching with love and mortification, would she have stooped down and kissed me if I had not been a little boy. How I despised little boys ! How I hated one particular little boy — too little to be loved !

I smile over this very grimly even now. My

sorrow was genuine and bitter. It is a great mistake on the part of elderly ladies, male and female,
to tell a child that he is seeing his happiest days.
Do not you believe a word of it, my little friend.
The burdens of childhood are as hard to bear as
the crosses that weigh us down later in life, while
the happinesses of childhood are tame compared
with those of our maturer years. And even if
this were not so, it is rank cruelty to throw
shadows over the young heart by croaking, "Be
merry, for to-morrow you die!"

As the last days of Nellie's visit drew near, I
fell into a very unhealthy state of mind. To have
her so frank and unconsciously coquettish with
me was a daily torment; to be looked upon and
treated as a child was bitter almonds; but the
thought of losing her altogether was distraction.

The summer was at an end. The days were
perceptibly shorter, and now and then came an
evening when it was chilly enough to have a wood
fire in our sitting-room. The leaves were beginning to take hectic tints, and the wind was prac-
ticing the minor pathetic notes of its autumnal
dirge. Nature and myself appeared to be approaching our dissolution simultaneously.

One evening, the evening previous to the day
set for Nelly's departure — how well I remember
it! — I found her sitting alone by the wide chim-
ney-piece looking musingly at the crackling back-
log. There were no candles in the room. On

The Last Evening

her face and hands, and on the small golden cross
at her throat, fell the flickering firelight — that
ruddy, mellow firelight in which one's grandmother would look poetical.

I drew a low stool from the corner and placed
it by the side of her chair. She reached out her
hand to me, as was her pretty fashion, and so we
sat for several moments silently in the changing

glow of the burning logs.   Presently I moved back the stool so that I could see her face in profile without being seen by her.   I lost her hand by this movement, but I could not have spoken with the listless touch of her fingers on mine.   After two or three attempts I said "Nelly" a good deal louder than I intended.

Perhaps the effort it cost me was evident in my voice.   She raised herself quickly in the chair and half turned towards me.

"Well, Tom?"

"I — I am very sorry you are going away."

"So am I.   I have enjoyed every hour of my visit."

"Do you think you will ever come back here?"

"Perhaps," said Nelly, and her eyes wandered off into the fitful firelight.

"I suppose you will forget us all very quickly."

"Indeed I shall not.   I shall always have the pleasantest recollections of Rivermouth."

Here the conversation died a natural death. Nelly sank into a sort of dream, and I meditated. Fearing every moment to be interrupted by some member of the family, I nerved myself to make a bold dash.

"Nelly."

"Well."

"Do you" — I hesitated.

"Do I what?"

"Love any one very much?"

"Why, of course I do," said Nelly, scattering her revery with a merry laugh. "I love Uncle Nutter and Aunt Nutter, and you — and Towser."

Towser, our new dog! I could not stand that. I pushed back the stool impatiently and stood in front of her.

"That's not what I mean," I said angrily.

"Well, what do you mean?"

"Do you love any one to marry him?"

"The idea of it," cried Nelly, laughing.

"But you must tell me."

"Must, Tom?"

"Indeed you must, Nelly."

She had risen from the chair with an amused, perplexed look in her eyes. I held her an instant by the dress.

"Please tell me."

"Oh you silly boy!" cried Nelly. Then she rumpled my hair all over my forehead and ran laughing out of the room.

Suppose Cinderella had rumpled the prince's hair all over his forehead, how would he have liked it? Suppose the Sleeping Beauty when the king's son with a kiss set her and all the old clocks agoing in the spellbound castle — suppose the young minx had looked up and coolly laughed in his eye, I guess the king's son would not have been greatly pleased.

I hesitated a second or two and then rushed after Nelly just in time to run against Miss Abigail, who entered the room with a couple of lighted candles.

"Goodness gracious, Tom!" exclaimed Miss Abigail, "*are* you possessed?"

I left her scraping the warm spermaceti from one of her thumbs.

Nelly was in the kitchen talking quite unconcernedly with Kitty Collins. There she remained until supper-time. Supper over, we all adjourned to the sitting-room. I planned and plotted, but could manage in no way to get Nelly alone. She and the Captain played cribbage all the evening.

The next morning my lady did not make her appearance until we were seated at the breakfast-table. I had got up at daylight myself. Immediately after breakfast the carriage arrived to take her to the railway station. A

Removing the Spermaceti

gentleman stepped from this carriage, and greatly to my surprise was warmly welcomed by the Captain and Miss Abigail, and by Miss Nelly herself, who seemed unnecessarily glad to see him. From the hasty conversation that followed I learned that the gentleman had come somewhat unexpectedly to conduct Miss Nelly to Boston. But how did he know that she was to leave that morning? Nelly bade farewell to the Captain and Miss Abigail, made a little rush and kissed me on the nose, and was gone.

As the wheels of the hack rolled up the street and over my finer feelings, I turned to the Captain.

"Who was that gentleman, sir?"

"That was Mr. Waldron."

"A relation of yours, sir?" I asked craftily.

"No relation of mine — a relation of Nelly's," said the Captain, smiling.

"A cousin," I suggested, feeling a strange hatred spring up in my bosom for the unknown.

"Well, I suppose you might call him a cousin for the present. He's going to marry little Nelly next summer."

In one of Peter Parley's valuable historical works is a description of an earthquake at Lisbon. "At the first shock the inhabitants rushed into the streets; the earth yawned at their feet and the houses tottered and fell on every side." I staggered past the Captain into the street; a giddiness came over me; the earth yawned at my feet, and the houses threatened to fall in on every side of me. How distinctly I remember that momentary sense of confusion when everything in the world seemed toppling over into ruins.

As I have remarked, my love for Nelly is a thing of the past. I had not thought of her for years until I sat down to write this chapter, and yet, now that all is said and done, I should not care particularly to come across Mrs. Waldron's eldest boy in my afternoon's walk. He must be fourteen or fifteen years old by this time — the young villain!

CHAPTER XIX

I BECOME A BLIGHTED BEING

WHEN a young boy gets to be an old boy, when the hair is growing rather thin on the top of the old boy's head, and he has been tamed sufficiently to take a sort of chastened pleasure in allowing the baby to play with his watch-seals — when, I say, an old boy has reached this stage in the journey of life, he is sometimes apt to indulge in sportive remarks concerning his first love.

Now, though I bless my stars that it was not in my power to marry Miss Nelly, I am not going to deny my boyish regard for her nor laugh at it. As long as it lasted it was a very sincere and unselfish love, and rendered me proportionately wretched. I say as long as it lasted, for one's first love does not last forever.

I am ready, however, to laugh at the amusing figure I cut after I had really ceased to have any deep feeling in the matter. It was then I took it into my head to be a Blighted Being. This was about two weeks after the spectral appearance of Mr. Waldron.

For a boy of a naturally vivacious disposition, the part of a blighted being presented difficulties.

I had an excellent appetite, I liked society, I liked out-of-door sports, I was fond of handsome clothes. Now all these things were incompatible with the doleful character I was to assume, and I proceeded to cast them from me.

I neglected my hair. I avoided my play-mates. I frowned ab-stractedly. I did not eat as much as was good for me. I took lonely walks. I brood-ed in solitude. I not only committed to memory the more tur-

In Love

gid poems of the late Lord Byron—"Fare thee well, and if forever," etc.—but I became a de-spondent poet on my own account, and composed a string of "Stanzas to One who will understand them." I think I was a trifle too hopeful on that point; for I came across the verses several years afterwards, and was quite unable to understand them myself.

It was a great comfort to be so perfectly miser-able and yet not suffer any. I used to look in the glass and gloat over the amount and variety of mournful expressions I could throw into my fea-tures. If I caught myself smiling at anything, I cut the smile short with a sigh. The oddest thing about all this is, I never once suspected that I was *not* unhappy. No one, not even Pepper Whitcomb, was more deceived than I.

Among the minor pleasures of being blighted were the interest and perplexity I excited in the simple souls that were thrown in daily contact with me. Pepper especially. I nearly drove him into a corresponding state of mind.

I had from time to time given Pepper slight but impressive hints of my admiration for Some One (this was in the early part of Miss Glentworth's visit) ; I had also led him to infer that my admiration was not altogether in vain. He was therefore unable to explain the cause of my strange behavior, for I had carefully refrained from mentioning to Pepper the fact that Some One had turned out to be Another's.

I treated Pepper shabbily. I could not resist playing on his tenderer feelings. He was a boy bubbling over with sympathy for any one in any kind of trouble. Our intimacy since Binny Wallace's death had been uninterrupted ; but now I moved in a sphere apart, not to be profaned by the step of an outsider.

I no longer joined the boys on the playground at recess. I stayed at my desk reading some lugubrious volume — usually The Mysteries of Udolpho, by the amiable Mrs. Radcliffe. A translation of The Sorrows of Werther fell into my hands at this period, and if I could have committed suicide without killing myself, I should certainly have done so.

On half-holidays, instead of fraternizing with Pepper and the rest of our clique, I would wander off alone to Grave Point.

Grave Point — the place where Binny Wallace's body came ashore — was a narrow strip of land running out into the river. A line of Lombardy poplars, stiff and severe, like a row of grenadiers, mounted guard on the water-side. On the extreme end of the peninsula was an old disused graveyard, tenanted principally by the early settlers who had been scalped by the Indians. In a remote corner of the cemetery, set apart from the other mounds, was the grave of a woman who had been hanged in the old colonial times for the murder of her infant. Goodwife Polly Haines had denied the crime to the last, and after her death there had arisen strong doubts as to her actual guilt. It was a belief current among the lads of the town, that if you went to this grave at night-fall on the 10th of November — the anniversary of her execution — and asked, " For what did the magistrates hang you?" a voice would reply, " Nothing."

Many a Rivermouth boy has tremblingly put this question in the dark, and, sure enough, Polly Haines invariably answered nothing!

A low red-brick wall, broken down in many places and frosted over with silvery moss, surrounded this burial-ground of our Pilgrim Fathers and their immediate descendants. The latest date

on any of the headstones was 1760. A crop of
very funny epitaphs sprung up here and there
among the overgrown thistles and burdocks, and
almost every tablet had a death's-head with cross-
bones engraved upon it, or else a puffy round face
with a pair of wings stretching out from the ears,
like this :

These mortuary emblems furnished me with
congenial food for reflection.   I used to lie in the
long grass, and speculate on the advantages and
disadvantages of being a cherub.

I forget what I thought the advantages were,
but I remember distinctly of getting into an inex-
tricable tangle on two points : How could a cherub,
being all head and wings, manage to sit down
when he was tired ?   To have to sit down on the
back of his head struck me as an awkward alter-
native.   Again : Where did a cherub carry those
indispensable articles (such as jackknives, marbles,
and pieces of twine) which boys in an earthly state
of existence usually stow away in their trousers
pockets ?

These were knotty questions, and I was never
able to dispose of them satisfactorily.

I am a Blighted Being

Meanwhile Pepper Whitcomb would scour the whole town in search of me. He finally discovered my retreat, and dropped in on me abruptly one afternoon, while I was deep in the cherub problem.

"Look here, Tom Bailey!" said Pepper, shying a piece of clam-shell indignantly at the *Hic jacet* on a neighboring gravestone, "you are just going to the dogs! Can't you tell a fellow what in thunder ails you, instead of prowling round among the tombs like a jolly old vampire?"

"Pepper," I replied, solemnly, "don't ask me; you would n't understand. Some day you may. You are too fat and thoughtless now."

Pepper stared at me.

"Earthly happiness," I continued, "is a delusion and a snare. You will never be happy, Pepper, until you are a cherub."

Pepper, by the by, would have made an excellent cherub, he was so chubby. Having delivered myself of these gloomy remarks, I arose languidly from the grass and moved away, leaving Pepper staring after me in mute astonishment. I was Hamlet and Werther and the late Lord Byron all in one.

You will ask what my purpose was in cultivating this factitious despondency. None whatever. Blighted Beings never have any purpose in life excepting to be as blighted as possible.

Of course my present line of business could not

long escape the eye of Captain Nutter. I do not
know if the Captain suspected my attachment for
Miss Glentworth. He never alluded to it; but
he watched me. Miss Abigail watched me, Kitty
Collins watched me, and Sailor Ben watched me.

" I can't make out his signals," I overheard the
Admiral remark to my grandfather one day. " I
hope he ain't got no kind of sickness aboard."

There was something singularly agreeable in
being an object of so great interest. Sometimes
I had all I could do to preserve my dejected aspect, it was so pleasant to be miserable. I incline
to the opinion that persons who are melancholy
without any particular reason, such as poets, ar-
tists, and young musicians with long hair, have
rather an enviable time of it. In a quiet way I
never enjoyed myself better in my life than when
I was a Blighted Being.

CHAPTER XX

IT was not possible for a boy of my temper-
ament to be a blighted being longer than three
consecutive weeks.

I was gradually emerging from my self-imposed
cloud when events took place that greatly assisted
in restoring me to a more natural frame of mind.
I awoke from an imaginary trouble to face a real
one.

I suppose you do not know what a financial
crisis is ? I will give you an illustration.

You are deeply in debt — say to the amount of
a quarter of a dollar — to the little knicknack shop
round the corner, where they sell picture-papers,
spruce-gum, needles, and Malaga raisins. A boy
owes you a quarter of a dollar, which he promises
to pay at a certain time. You are depending on
this quarter to settle accounts with the small
shopkeeper. The time arrives — and the quarter
does not. That 's a financial crisis, in one sense
— in twenty-five senses, if I may say so.

When this same thing happens, on a grander
scale, in the mercantile world, it produces what is

called a panic. One man's inability to pay his debts ruins another man, who, in turn, ruins some one else, and so on, until failure after failure makes even the richest capitalists tremble. Public confidence is suspended, and the smaller fry of merchants are knocked over like tenpins.

These commercial panics occur periodically, after the fashion of comets and earthquakes and other disagreeable things. Such a panic took place in New Orleans in the year 18— and my father's banking-house went to pieces in the crash.

Of a comparatively large fortune nothing remained after paying his debts excepting a few thousand dollars, with which he proposed to return North and embark in some less hazardous enterprise. In the mean time it was necessary for him to stay in New Orleans to wind up the business.

My grandfather was in some way involved in this failure, and lost, I fancy, a considerable sum of money ; but he never talked much on the subject. He was an unflinching believer in the spilt-milk proverb.

" It can't be gathered up," he would say, "and it 's no use crying over it. Pitch into the cow and get some more milk, is my motto."

The suspension of the banking-house was bad enough, but there was an attending circumstance that gave us, at Rivermouth, a great deal more anxiety. The cholera, which some one predicted would visit the country that year, and which, indeed, had made its appearance in a mild form at several points along the Mississippi River, had broken out with much violence at New Orleans.

The report that first reached us through the newspapers was meagre and contradictory ; many persons discredited it ; but a letter from my mother left us no room for doubt. The sickness was in the city. The hospitals were filling up, and hundreds of the citizens were flying from the stricken place by every steamboat. The unsettled state of my father's affairs made it imperative for him to remain at his post ; his desertion at that moment would have been at the sacrifice of all he had saved from the general wreck.

As he would be detained in New Orleans at least three months, my mother declined to come North without him.

After this we awaited with feverish impatience the weekly news that came to us from the South. The next letter advised us that my parents were well, and that the sickness, so far, had not penetrated to the faubourg, or district, where they lived. The following week brought less cheering tidings. My father's business, in consequence of the flight of the other partners, would keep him in the city beyond the period he had mentioned. The family had moved to Pass Christian, a favorite watering-place on Lake Pontchartrain, near New Orleans, where he was able to spend part of each week. So the return North was postponed indefinitely.

It was now that the old longing to see my parents came back to me with irresistible force. I knew my grandfather would not listen to the idea of my going to New Orleans at such a dangerous time, since he had opposed the journey so strongly when the same objection did not exist. But I determined to go nevertheless.

I think I have mentioned the fact that all the male members of our family, on my father's side — as far back as the Middle Ages — have exhibited in early youth a decided talent for running away. It was an hereditary talent. It ran in the blood to run away. I do not pretend to explain the peculiarity. I simply admit it.

It was not my fate to change the prescribed order of things. I, too, was to run away, thereby proving, if any proof were needed, that I was the grandson of my grandfather. I do not hold myself responsible for the step any more than I do for the shape of my nose, which is said to be a fac-simile of Captain Nutter's.

I have frequently noticed how circumstances conspire to help a man, or a boy, when he has thoroughly resolved on doing a thing. That very week the Rivermouth Barnacle printed an advertisement that seemed to have been written on purpose for me. It read as follows :

WANTED.— A Few ABLE-BODIED SEAMEN and a Cabin-Boy, for the ship *Rawlings*, now loading for New Orleans at Johnson's Wharf, Boston.   Apply in person, within four days, at the office of Messrs. ——— ——— & Co., or on board the Ship.

How I was to get to New Orleans with only $4.62 was a question that had been bothering me. This advertisement made it as clear as day. I would go as cabin-boy.

I had taken Pepper into my confidence again; I had told him the story of my love for Miss Glentworth, with all its harrowing details ; and now conceived it judicious to confide in him the change about to take place in my life, so that, if the Rawlings went down in a gale, my friends might have the limited satisfaction of knowing what had become of me.

Pepper shook his head discouragingly, and sought in every way to dissuade me from the step. He drew a disenchanting picture of the existence of a cabin-boy, whose constant duty (according to Pepper) was to have dishes broken over his head whenever the captain or the mate chanced to be out of humor, which was mostly all the time. But nothing Pepper said could turn me a hair's breadth from my purpose.

I had little time to spare, for the advertisement stated explicity that applications were to be made in person within four days. I trembled to think of the bare possibility of some other boy snapping up that desirable situation.

It was on Monday that I stumbled upon the

advertisement.   On   Tuesday   my   preparations
were   completed.   My   baggage — consisting   of
four shirts, half a dozen collars, a piece of shoe-
maker's wax (Heaven knows what for !), and five
stockings, wrapped in a silk handkerchief — lay
hidden under a loose plank of the stable floor.
This was my point of departure.

My plan was to take the last train for Boston,
in order to prevent the possibility of immediate
pursuit, if any should be attempted.   The train
left at 4 P. M.

I ate no breakfast and little dinner that day.   I
avoided the Captain's eye, and would not have
looked Miss Abigail or Kitty in the face for the
wealth of the Indies.

When it was time to start for the station I retired quietly to the stable and uncovered my bundle.   I lingered a moment to kiss the white star
on Gypsy's forehead, and was nearly unmanned
when the little animal returned the caress by lapping my cheek.   Twice I went back and patted
her.

On reaching the station I purchased my ticket
with a bravado air that ought to have aroused the
suspicion of the ticket-master, and hurried to the
car, where I sat fidgeting until the train shot out
into the broad daylight.

Then I drew a long breath and looked about
me.   The first object that saluted my sight was
Sailor Ben, four or five seats behind me, reading
the Rivermouth Barnacle !

Reading was not an easy art to Sailor Ben ; he grappled with the sense of a paragraph as if it were a polar bear, and generally got the worst of it. On the present occasion he was having a hard struggle, judging by the way he worked his mouth and rolled his eyes. He had evidently not seen me. But what was he doing on the Boston train ?

Without lingering to solve the question, I stole gently from my seat and passed into the forward car.

This was very awkward, having the Admiral on board. I could not understand it at all. Could it be possible that the old boy had got tired of land and was running away to sea himself ? That was too absurd a supposition. I glanced nervously towards the car door now and then, half expecting to see him come after me.

We had passed one or two way-stations, and I had quieted down a good deal, when I began to feel as if somebody was looking steadily at the back of my head. I turned round involuntarily and there was Sailor Ben again, at the farther end of the car, wrestling with the Rivermouth Barnacle as before.

I began to grow very uncomfortable indeed. Was it by design or chance that he thus dogged my steps ? If he was aware of my presence, why did he not speak to me at once ? Why did he steal round, making no sign, like a particularly unpleasant phantom ? Maybe it *was not* Sailor

Ben. I peeped at him slyly. There was no mistaking that tanned, genial phiz of his. Very odd he did not see *me!*

Literature, even in the mild form of a country newspaper, always had the effect of poppies on the Admiral. When I stole another glance in his direction his hat was tilted over his right eye in the most dissolute style, and the Rivermouth Barnacle lay in a confused heap beside him. He had succumbed. He was fast asleep. If he would only keep asleep until we reached our destination!

The Admiral on Guard

By and by I discovered that the rear car had been detached from the train at the last stopping-place. This accounted satisfactorily for Sailor Ben's singular movements, and considerably calmed my fears. Nevertheless, I did not like the aspect of things.

The Admiral continued to snooze like a good fellow, and was snoring melodiously as we glided at a slackened pace over a bridge and into Boston.

I grasped my pilgrim's bundle, and, hurrying out of the car, dashed up the first street that presented itself.

It was a narrow, noisy, zigzag street, crowded with trucks and obstructed with bales and boxes of merchandise. I did not pause to breathe until I had placed a respectable distance between me and the railway station. By this time it was nearly twilight.

I had got into the region of dwelling-houses, and was about to seat myself on a doorstep to rest, when, lo! there was the Admiral trundling along on the opposite sidewalk, under a full spread of canvas, as he would have expressed it.

I was off again in an instant at a rapid pace; but in spite of all I could do he held his own without any perceptible exertion. He had a very ugly gait to get away from, the Admiral. I did not dare to run, for fear of being mistaken for a thief, a suspicion which my bundle would naturally lend color to.

I pushed ahead, however, at a brisk trot, and must have got over one or two miles — my pursuer neither gaining nor losing ground — when I concluded to surrender at discretion. I saw that Sailor Ben was determined to have me, and, knowing my man, I knew that escape was highly improbable.

So I turned round and waited for him to catch up with me, which he did in a few seconds, looking rather sheepish at first.

" Sailor Ben," said I severely, " do I understand that you are dogging my steps ? "

" Well, little messmate," replied the Admiral, rubbing his nose, which he always did when he was disconcerted, "I *am* kind o' followin' in your wake."

" Under orders ? "

" Under orders."

" Under the Captain's orders ? "

" Surely."

" In other words, my grandfather has sent you to fetch me back to Rivermouth ? "

" That's about it," said the Admiral, with a burst of frankness.

" And I must go with you whether I want to or not ? "

" The Capen's very identical words ! "

There was nothing to be done. I bit my lips with suppressed anger, and signified that I was at his disposal, since I could not help it. The impression was very strong in my mind that the Admiral would not hesitate to put me in irons if I showed signs of mutiny.

It was too late to return to Rivermouth that night — a fact which I communicated to the old boy sullenly, inquiring at the same time what he proposed to do about it.

He said we would cruise about for some rations, and then make a night of it. I did not condescend to reply, though I hailed the suggestion of something to eat with inward enthusiasm, for I had not taken enough food that day to keep life in a canary.

We wandered back to the railway station, in the waiting-room of which was a kind of restaurant presided over by a severe - looking young lady. Here we had a cup of coffee apiece, several tough doughnuts, and some blocks of venerable sponge-cake. The young lady who attended on us, whatever her age was then, must have been a mere child when that sponge-cake was made.

The Admiral's acquaintance with Boston hotels was slight; but he knew of a quiet lodging-house near by, much patronized by sea-captains, and kept by a former friend of his.

In this house, which had seen its best days, we were accommodated with a mouldy chamber containing two cot-beds, two chairs, and a cracked pitcher on a washstand. The mantel-shelf was ornamented with three big pink conch-shells, resembling pieces of petrified liver; and over these hung a cheap lurid print, in which a United States sloop-of-war was giving a British frigate particular fits. It is very strange how our own ships never seem to suffer any in these terrible engagements. It shows what a nation we are.

An oil-lamp on a deal-table cast a dismal glare over the apartment, which was cheerless in the extreme. I thought of our sitting-room at home, with its flowery wall-paper and gay curtains and soft lounges; I saw Major Elkanah Nutter (my grandfather's father) in powdered wig and Federal uniform, looking down benevolently from his

gilt frame between the bookcases; I pictured
the Captain and Miss Abigail sitting at the cosy
round table in the moonlight glow of the astral
lamp; and then I fell to wondering how they
would receive me when I came back. I wondered
if the Prodigal Son had any idea that his father
was going to kill the fatted calf for him, and how
he felt about it, on the whole.

Though I was very low in spirits, I put on a
bold front to Sailor Ben, you will understand. To
be caught and caged in this manner was a fright-
ful shock to my vanity. He tried to draw me into
conversation; but I answered in icy monosyllables.
He again suggested we should make a night of
it, and hinted broadly that he was game for any
amount of riotous dissipation, even to the extent
of going to see a play if I wanted to. I declined
haughtily. I was dying to go.

He then threw out a feeler on the subject of
dominoes and checkers, and observed in a general
way that "seven up" was a capital game; but I
repulsed him at every point.

I saw that the Admiral was beginning to feel
hurt by my systematic coldness. We had always
been such hearty friends until now. It was too
bad of me to fret that tender, honest old heart
even for an hour. I really did love the ancient
boy, and when in a disconsolate way he ordered
up a pitcher of beer, I unbent so far as to partake
of some in a teacup. He recovered his spirits

instantly, and took out his cuddy clay pipe for a smoke.

Between the beer and the soothing fragrance of the navy-plug, I fell into a pleasanter mood myself, and, it being too late now to go to the

Playing " Seven Up "

theatre, I condescended to say — addressing the northwest corner of the ceiling — that " seven up " *was* a capital game. Upon this hint the Admiral disappeared, and returned shortly with a very dirty pack of cards.

As we played, with varying fortunes, by the

flickering flame of the lamp, he sipped his beer and became communicative. He seemed immensely tickled by the fact that I had come to Boston. It leaked out presently that he and the Captain had had a wager on the subject.

The discovery of my plans and who had discovered them were points on which the Admiral refused to throw any light. They had been discovered, however, and the Captain had laughed at the idea of my running away. Sailor Ben, on the contrary, had stoutly contended that I meant to slip cable and be off. Whereupon the captain offered to bet him a dollar that I would not go. And it was partly on account of this wager that Sailor Ben refrained from capturing me when he might have done so at the start.

Now, as the fare to and from Boston, with the lodging expenses, would cost at least five dollars, I did not see what he gained by winning the wager. The Admiral rubbed his nose violently when this view of the case presented itself.

I asked him why he did not take me from the train at the first stopping-place and return to Rivermouth by the down train at 4.30. He explained : having purchased a ticket for Boston, he considered himself bound to the owners (the stockholders of the road) to fulfill his part of the contract. To use his own words, he had "shipped for the viage."

This struck me as being so deliciously funny, that

after I was in bed and the light was out I could not help laughing aloud once or twice. I suppose the Admiral must have thought I was meditating another escape, for he made periodical visits to my bed throughout the night, satisfying himself by kneading me all over that I had not evaporated.

I was all there the next morning, when Sailor Ben half awakened me by shouting merrily, " All hands on deck ! " The words rang in my ears like a part of my own dream, for I was at that instant climbing up the side of the Rawlings to offer myself as cabin-boy.

The Admiral was obliged to shake me roughly two or three times before he could detach me from the dream. I opened my eyes with effort, and stared stupidly round the room. Bit by bit my real situation dawned on me. What a sickening sensation that is, when one is in trouble, to wake up feeling free for a moment, and then to find yesterday's sorrow all ready to go on again !

" Well, little messmate, how fares it ? "

I was too much depressed to reply. The thought of returning to Rivermouth chilled me. How could I face Captain Nutter, to say nothing of Miss Abigail and Kitty ? How the Temple Grammar School boys would look at me ! How Conway and Seth Rodgers would exult over my mortification ! And what if the Rev. Wibird Hawkins should allude to me in his next Sunday's sermon ?

Sailor Ben was wise in keeping an eye on me, for after these thoughts took possession of my mind, I wanted only the opportunity to give him the slip.

The keeper of the lodgings did not supply meals to his guests ; so we breakfasted at a small chop-house in a crooked street on our way to the cars. The city was not astir yet, and looked glum and careworn in the damp morning atmosphere.

Here and there as we passed along was a sharp-faced shop-boy taking down shutters ; and now and then we met a seedy man who had evidently spent the night in a doorway. Such early birds and a few laborers with their tin kettles were the only signs of life to be seen until we came to the station, where I insisted on paying for my own ticket. I did not relish being conveyed from place to place, like a felon changing prisons, at somebody else's expense.

On entering the car I sunk into a seat next the window, and Sailor Ben deposited himself beside me, cutting off all chance of escape.

The car filled up soon after this, and I wondered if there was anything in my mien that would lead the other passengers to suspect I was a boy who had run away and was being brought back.

A man in front of us — he was near-sighted, as I discovered later by his reading a guide-book with his nose — brought the blood to my cheeks by turning round and peering at me steadily. I rubbed a clear spot on the cloudy window-glass at my elbow, and looked out to avoid him.

There, in the travelers' room, was the severe-looking young lady piling up her blocks of sponge-cake in alluring pyramids and industriously intrenching herself behind a breastwork of squash-pie. I saw with pleasure numerous victims walk up to the counter and recklessly sow the seeds of death in their constitutions by eating her doughnuts. I had got quite interested in her, when the whistle sounded and the train began to move.

The Near-Sighted Man

The Admiral and I did not talk much on the journey. I stared out of the window most of the time, speculating as to the probable nature of the reception in store for me at the terminus of the road.

What would the Captain say? and Mr. Grimshaw, what would he do about it? Then I thought of Pepper Whitcomb. Dire was the vengeance I meant to wreak on Pepper, for who but he had

betrayed me? Pepper alone had been the reposi-
tory of my secret —perfidious Pepper!

As we left station after station behind us, I felt
less and less like encountering the members of
our family. Sailor Ben fathomed what was passing in my mind, for he leaned over and said :

" I don't think as the Capen will bear down very
hard on you."

But it was not that. It was not the fear of any
physical punishment that might be inflicted ; it
was the sense of my own folly that was creeping
over me ; for during the long, silent ride I had
examined my conduct from every standpoint, and
there was no view I could take of myself in which
I did not look like a very foolish person indeed.

As we came within sight of the spires of Rivermouth, I would not have cared if the up train,
which met us outside the town, had run into us
and ended me.

Contrary to my expectation and dread, the Captain was not visible when we stepped from the
cars. Sailor Ben glanced among the crowd of
faces, apparently looking for him too. Conway
was there — he was always hanging about the station — and if he had intimated in any way that he
knew of my disgrace and enjoyed it, I should
have walked into him, I am certain.

But this defiant feeling entirely deserted me by
the time we reached the Nutter House. The
Captain himself opened the door.

"Come on board, sir," said Sailor Ben, scraping his left foot and touching his hat sea-fashion.

My grandfather nodded to Sailor Ben, somewhat coldly I thought, and much to my astonishment kindly took me by the hand.

I was unprepared for this, and the tears, which no amount of severity would have wrung from me, welled up to my eyes.

The expression of my grandfather's face, as I glanced at it hastily, was grave and gentle; there was nothing in it of anger or reproof. I followed him into the sitting-room, and, obeying a motion of his hand, seated myself on the sofa. He remained standing by the round table for a moment, lost in thought, then leaned over and picked up a letter.

It was a letter with a great black seal.

CHAPTER XXI

IN WHICH I LEAVE RIVERMOUTH

A LETTER with a great black seal!

I knew then what had happened as well as I know it now. But which was it, father or mother? I do not like to look back to the agony and suspense of that moment.

My father had died at New Orleans during one of his weekly visits to the city. The letter bearing these tidings had reached Rivermouth the evening of my flight — had passed me on the road by the down train.

I must turn back for a moment to that eventful evening. When I failed to make my appearance at supper, the Captain began to suspect that I had really started on my wild tour southward — a conjecture which Sailor Ben's absence helped to confirm. I had evidently got off by the train and Sailor Ben had followed me.

There was no telegraphic communication between Boston and Rivermouth in those days; so my grandfather could do nothing but await the result. Even if there had been another mail to Boston, he could not have availed himself of it, not knowing how to address a message to the fugitives. The post-office was naturally the last place either I or the Admiral would think of visiting.

My grandfather, however, was too full of trouble to allow this to add to his distress. He knew that the faithful old sailor would not let me come to any harm, and even if I had managed for the time being to elude him, was sure to bring me back sooner or later.

On our return, therefore, by the first train on the following day did not surprise him.

I was greatly puzzled, as I have said, by the gentle manner of his reception ; but when we were alone together in the sitting-room, and he began slowly to unfold the letter, I understood it all. I caught a sight of my mother's handwriting in the superscription, and there was nothing left to tell me.

My grandfather held the letter a few seconds irresolutely, and then commenced reading it aloud ; but he could get no further than the date.

"I can't read it, Tom," said the old gentleman, breaking down. "I thought I could."

He handed it to me. I took the letter mechanically, and hurried away with it to my little room, where I had passed so many happy hours.

The week that followed the receipt of this letter is nearly a blank in my memory. I remember that the days appeared endless ; that at times I could not realize the misfortune that had befallen us, and my heart upbraided me for not feeling a deeper grief; that a full sense of my loss would now and then sweep over me like an inspiration, and I would steal away to my chamber or wander forlornly about the gardens. I remember this, but little more.

As the days went by my first grief subsided, and in its place grew up a want which I have experienced at every step in life from boyhood to manhood. Often, even now, after all these years,

My First Grief

when I see a lad of twelve or fourteen walking by his father's side, and glancing merrily up at his face, I turn and look after them, and am conscious that I have missed companionship most sweet and sacred.

I shall not dwell on this portion of my story. There were many tranquil, pleasant hours in store for me at that period, and I prefer to turn to them.

One evening the Captain came smiling into the sitting-room with an open letter in his hand. My mother had arrived at New York, and would be with us the next day. For the first time in weeks — years, it seemed to me — something of the old cheerfulness mingled with our conversation round the evening lamp. I was to go to Boston with the Captain to meet her and bring her home. I need not describe that meeting. With my mother's hand in mine once more, all the long years we had been parted appeared like a dream. Very dear to me was the sight of that slender, pale woman passing from room to room, and lending a patient grace and beauty to the saddened life of the old house.

Everything was changed with us now. There were consultations with lawyers, and signing of papers, and correspondence ; for my father's affairs had been left in great confusion. And when these were settled, the evenings were not long enough for us to hear all my mother had to tell of the scenes she had passed through in the ill-fated city.

Then there were old times to talk over, full of reminiscences of Aunt Chloe and little Black Sam. Little Black Sam, by the by, had been taken by his master from my father's service ten months previously, and put on a sugar-plantation near Baton Rouge. Not relishing the change, Sam had run away, and by some mysterious agency got into Canada, from which place he had sent back several indecorous messages to his late owner. Aunt Chloe was still in New Orleans, employed as nurse in one of the cholera hospital wards, and the Desmoulins, near neighbors of ours, had purchased the pretty brick house among the orange-trees.

How all these simple details interested me will be readily understood by any boy who has been long absent from home.

I was sorry when it became necessary to discuss questions more nearly affecting myself. I had been removed from school temporarily, but it was decided, after much consideration, that I should not return, the decision being left, in a manner, in my own hands.

The Captain wished to carry out his son's intention and send me to college, as I was fully prepared to undergo the preliminary examinations. This, however, would have been a heavy drain on the modest income reverting to my mother after the settlement of my father's estate, and the Captain proposed to take the expense upon himself, not seeing clearly what other disposal to make of me.

In the midst of our discussions a letter came from my Uncle Snow, a merchant in New York, generously offering me a place in his counting-house. The case resolved itself into this: If I went to college, I should have to devote several years to my studies, and at the end of the collegiate course would have no settled profession. If I accepted my uncle's offer, which could not stand waiting, I should at once be in a comparatively independent position. It was hard to give up the long-cherished dream of being a Harvard boy; but I gave it up.

The decision once made, it was Uncle Snow's wish that I should enter his counting-house immediately. The cause of my good uncle's haste was this: he was afraid that I would turn out to be a poet before he could make a merchant of me.

His fears were based upon the fact that I had published in the Rivermouth Barnacle some verses addressed in a familiar manner "To the Moon." Now, the idea of a boy, with his living to get, placing himself in communication with the Moon, struck the mercantile mind as monstrous. It was not only a bad investment, it was lunacy.

We adopted Uncle Snow's views so far as to accede to his proposition forthwith. My mother, I neglected to say, was also to reside in New York.

I shall not draw a picture of Pepper Whitcomb's disgust when the news was imparted to him, nor attempt to paint Sailor Ben's distress at the prospect of losing his little messmate.

In the excitement of preparing for the journey

I did not feel any very deep regret myself. But when the moment came for leaving, and I saw my small trunk lashed up behind the carriage, then the pleasantness of the old life and a vague dread of the new came over me, and a mist filled my eyes, shutting out the group of schoolfellows, including all the members of the Centipede Club, who had come down to the house to see me off.

As the carriage swept round the corner, I leaned out of the window to take a last look at Sailor Ben's cottage, and there was the Admiral's flag flying at half-mast.

So I left Rivermouth, little dreaming that I was not to see the old place again for many and many a year.

CHAPTER XXII

EXEUNT OMNES

WITH the close of my schooldays at Rivermouth this modest chronicle ends.

The new life upon which I entered, the new friends and foes I encountered on the road, and what I did and what I did not, are matters that do not come within the scope of these pages. But before I write Finis to the record as it stands, before I leave it — feeling as if I were once more going away from my boyhood — I have a word or two to say concerning a few of the personages who have figured in the story, if you will allow me to call Gypsy a personage.

I am sure that the reader who has followed me thus far will be willing to hear what became of her, and Sailor Ben and Miss Abigail and the Captain.

First about Gypsy. A month after my departure from Rivermouth the Captain informed me by letter that he had parted with the little mare, according to agreement. She had been sold to the ring-master of a traveling circus (I had stipulated on this disposal of her), and was about to set out on her travels. She did not disappoint my glowing anticipations, but became quite a celebrity in her way, by dancing the polka to slow music on a pine-board ball-room constructed for the purpose.

I chanced once, a long while afterwards, to be in a country town where her troupe was giving exhibitions; I even read the gaudily illumined show-bill, setting forth the accomplishments of

— but failed to recognize my dear little mustang girl behind those high-sounding titles, and so, alas! did not attend the performance. I hope all the

praises she received and all the spangled trappings she wore did not spoil her ; but I am afraid they did, for she was always over much given to the vanities of this world.

Miss Abigail regulated the domestic destinies of my grandfather's household until the day of her death, which Dr. Theophilus Tredick solemnly averred was hastened by the inveterate habit she had contracted of swallowing unknown quantities of hot-drops whenever she fancied herself out of sorts. Eighty-seven empty phials were found in a bonnet-box on a shelf in her bedroom closet.

The old house became very lonely when the family got reduced to Captain Nutter and Kitty ; and when Kitty passed away, my grandfather divided his time between Rivermouth and New York.

Sailor Ben did not long survive his little Irish lass, as he always fondly called her. At his demise, which took place about six years ago, he left his property in trust to the managers of a "Home for Aged Mariners." In his will, which was a very whimsical document — written by himself, and worded with much shrewdness, too — he warned the Trustees that when he got "aloft" he intended to keep his "weather eye" on them, and should send "a speritual shot across their bows" and bring them to, if they did n't treat the Aged Mariners handsomely.

He also expressed a wish to have his body

stitched up in a shotted hammock and dropped into the harbor; but as he did not strenuously insist on this, and as it was not in accordance with my grandfather's preconceived notions of Christian burial, the Admiral was laid to rest beside Kitty, in the Old South Burying Ground, with an anchor that would have delighted him neatly carved on his headstone.

I am sorry the fire has gone out in the old ship's stove in that sky-blue cottage at the head of the wharf; I am sorry they have taken down the flagstaff and painted over the port-holes; for I loved the old cabin as it was. They might have let it alone!

For several months after leaving Rivermouth I carried on a voluminous correspondence with Pepper Whitcomb; but it gradually dwindled down to a single letter a month, and then to none at all. But while he remained at the Temple Grammar School he kept me advised of the current gossip of the town and the doings of the Centipedes.

As one by one the boys left the academy — Adams, Harris, Marden, Blake, and Langdon — to seek their fortunes elsewhere, there was less to interest me in the old seaport; and when Pepper himself went to Philadelphia to read law, I had no one to give me an inkling of what was going on.

There was not much to go on, to be sure. Great events no longer considered it worth their while to honor so quiet a place. One Fourth of

July the Temple Grammar School burnt down —
set on fire, it was supposed, by an eccentric squib
that was seen to dart into an upper window — and
Mr. Grimshaw retired from public life, married,
"and lived happily ever after," as the story-books
say.

The Widow Conway, I am able to state, did not
succeed in enslaving Mr. Meeks, the apothecary,
who united himself clandestinely to one of Miss
Dorothy Gibbs's young ladies, and lost the patron-
age of Primrose Hall in consequence.

Young Conway went into the grocery business
with his ancient chum, Rodgers — RODGERS &
CONWAY! I read the sign only last summer when
I was down in Rivermouth, and had half a mind to
pop into the shop and shake hands with him, and
ask him if he wanted to fight. I contented myself, however, with flattening my nose against his
dingy shop-window, and beheld Conway, in red
whiskers and blue overalls, weighing out sugar for
a customer — giving him short weight, I would
bet anything!

I have reserved my pleasantest word for the last.
It is touching the Captain. The Captain is still
hale and rosy, and if he does not relate his exploit
in the war of 1812 as spiritedly as he used to, he
makes up by relating it more frequently and telling it differently every time. He passes his winters in New York and his summers in the Nutter
House, which threatens to prove a hard nut for

the destructive gentleman with the scythe and the
hour-glass, for the seaward gable has not yielded
a clapboard to the east wind these twenty years.
The Captain has now become the Oldest Inhabitant in Rivermouth, and so I do not laugh at the
Oldest Inhabitant any more, but pray in my heart
that he may occupy the post of honor for half a
century to come !

So ends the Story of a Bad Boy — but not such
a very bad boy, as I told you to begin with.